"What

He held her fa...
"I have some id...

Logan kissed Dakota on her neck, letting his hands roam over her body. He moved around to stand behind her. His fingers poised over her dress zipper. "May I?"

She leaned into his touch. "Please do."

Expecting to feel a little nervous, Dakota was not prepared for the rush of longing that infused her when he undid her dress. His hand slid inside the garment to touch her back and caress her skin with soft, circular strokes. After a few moments, he used both hands to ease her dress off her shoulders before kissing her right shoulder blade.

Dakota turned around and then wrapped her arms around his neck. She kissed him again before lowering her hands to his shirt and unbuttoning it. "My turn," she said, easing the material away from his body.

Unable to help herself, her fingers fluttered across his chest. The muscles underneath were hard and firm. Next, her fingers moved to the buckle on his pants. Soon they were standing together in their underwear. Emboldened, Dakota reached around and unhooked her bra. She was completely nude before he had uttered a word.

"You're the sexiest best friend I've ever had."

She lay back on the bed, motioning for him to follow. "I feel the same way."

Logan lay down beside her. He traced the lines of her body with his hands as though committing every curve to memory. When he was done with his exploration, he rested the palm of his hand on her heart.

Books by Lisa Watson

Harlequin Kimani Romance

Love Contract
Her Heart's Desire
Love by Design

LISA WATSON

is a native of Washington, D.C., and writes multicultural novels. Having her debut novel nominated for Best Contemporary Fiction inspired Lisa to continue creating engaging story lines and strong characters with universal appeal and a keen sense of humor. Lisa also loves traveling, so weaving beautiful destinations into the pages of her novels as lush backdrops or as the heritage of her characters is not uncommon.

Lisa's first series for Harlequin Kimani Romance, The Match Broker series, introduced readers to matchmaking guru Norma Jean Anderson, aka The Love Broker. Her goal is to have her son, Adrian, and everyone in his immediate circle of friends happily married—period.

Lisa works at a technology consulting firm and is the copublicist for the *RT Book Reviews* annual RT Booklovers Conventions.

Married for eighteen years, with two teenagers and a Maltipoo, Brinkley, Lisa lives outside Raleigh, N.C., and is avidly working on her next series. Visit her website: www.lisawatson.com.

Love
By
Design

LISA WATSON

HARLEQUIN® KIMANI™ ROMANCE

For Dalen… Your guidance is invaluable.

Recycling programs
for this product may
not exist in your area.

ISBN-13: 978-0-373-86375-4

Love by Design

Copyright © 2014 by Lisa Y. Watson

HARLEQUIN®

™ www.Harlequin.com

Printed in U.S.A.

Dear Reader,

Can a first love be rekindled after years of silence? That's what Dakota Carson has to decide when Logan Montague returns with a business proposition she can't refuse. It's an emotional time for Dakota—Logan was her best childhood friend and the only man she's ever loved. When he left, she was devastated. His return wreaks havoc, and despite Dakota's protestations of indifference, it's an adjustment.

Logan's never stopped loving Dakota. While familial obligations caused him to leave, it's not the whole story.

I hope you enjoy this Harlequin Kimani Romance story. It's my favorite in the series, and I know you'll enjoy these characters as much as I do!

Be inspired...

Lisa

Thanks to Lisa Lanier. Your keen eye is so invaluable to me. You are a wonderful beta reader, and I'm so grateful for your flashes of inspiration!

To Pat Simmons, my literary partner-in-crime and a great story-teller. You excel at keeping me on deadline—and word count!

To Renee Bernard, the newest link in my armor and an amazing author. Thank you so much for all your sage advice and support. The stars definitely aligned the day we met! I'll be eternally grateful that I took a "detour"!

My thanks to fellow author Michelle Lindo-Rice for making sure my characters' Patois was irie!

To my FB Divas, Anita Tann, Jackie Roberts and LaVerne Aslam! You ladies are always excited and supportive, and I thank you!

Prologue

"I'm going to lose her."

Logan Montague sat on the bench in Grant Park. His world had just been blown apart, and the shards that were once his hopes and dreams scattered to the four winds. He was leaving Chicago…immediately. The timing of his parents' decree could not have been worse. He stared down at the grass beneath his feet, but all he saw was time running out. What he wanted least in the world, working in the family business, was going to be his entire future.

He sensed the urgency in his parents, and he wished he could just ignore it and go his own way, but he could not, nor would he shirk his responsibilities to his family. He just wished things had turned out differently.

One disaster at Montague International had his family scrambling to do damage control. His father was insistent that the news of one of their directors suspected of sabotage and trying to jump ship to the competition had to remain out of the public eye at all cost. They could tell no one about it for fear of scandal and plummeting stock prices. It was bad enough having to leave, but not being able to tell Dakota Carson the truth of the situation was unacceptable.

A light of potential that had once burned bright within his heart was just extinguished. As much as it would kill him to do so, he would not tell his best friend the truth about why he was leaving. He had been in love with her for a while, but had yet to make his feelings known. He always assumed he would have time. It had just run out.

"Hey."

Logan looked up to see her smiling down at him.

"Hey."

Dakota sat next to him on the park bench. "Sorry I'm late. You can't believe the amount of time it took me to finish up the chores Granny set out for me. It's like she knew I was in a rush to come see you and found a million reasons why I had to stay." She laughed. "But I finished, and here I am."

Logan nodded.

"So, what did you want to do this afternoon? A movie? A walk through the park? What about a trip to Navy Pier, or a boat ride?"

"I can't," he replied. "I won't be able to stay as long as I'd hoped."

"Oh, well, that's okay," Dakota replied, wrapping her arm around his. "I'm glad to see you, no matter what."

Logan closed his eyes and sighed. "Koty, there's something I have to tell you."

She glanced up at him. "Okay. Shoot."

"I have to go away…to New York…for the summer. I'm…I leave in a few days."

She sat up and faced him. "What? New York? Well, that's not too far away. We can still see each other, right?"

He glanced away. "My father wants me to learn the family business. That's going to take up most of my time."

She laughed. "You're kidding, right?"

Logan shook his head. "No, Koty. I have an internship at Montague. It's an opportunity I can't pass up. It'll help me when I start working there after college."

"But…I thought you didn't want to work for the family business? You always said it wasn't for you."

"I know…but things change."

"That's a pretty big change, Logan. I don't understand why you're just now telling me. You're practically gone tomorrow, and you spring this on me now?"

"I'm sorry. I just found out about it myself. It's all arranged."

The hurt in Dakota's eyes caused Logan's heart to tighten.

"Well, this sucks."

"I'm sorry I couldn't tell you sooner."

Tears fell in earnest now. "It's not your fault. You didn't know, right?" She hugged him tightly. "I'm going to miss you, Logan—more than you know."

He breathed in her scent. She was the most important person in his life. The turmoil he felt at saying goodbye was almost more than he could bear. No, this was wrong. He had to level with her. She deserved the truth, no matter what he promised.

"Dakota, there's something you need to know. I—"

His cell phone chirped. Logan glanced down at the screen. It was a text message from his mother.

"I'm sorry, Koty, but I have to go."

"Oh." She stood up, her expression crestfallen.

"I'll call you later." He tried to muster a smile, but failed miserably. "Let me see you home."

"No, I want to walk for a while. I just… I can't believe you're leaving so soon, Logan."

He pushed the hair out of her eyes. "Me, either. There's so much I wanted us to do."

"Me, too." She turned to face him. "It's our last summer before college. I thought we'd have more time."

"Hey." He reached out and took her hand. "Don't cry, Koty."

"I can't help it, Logan. I feel like my heart's going to break."

"You think it's any different for me?" he said raggedly.

She hugged him tightly, and kissed him on the cheek. "I'll miss you."

"Koty…forget waiting. There's something I want to tell you."

She smiled. "I know what it is."

Logan sighed with relief. "You do?"

"Yes, and I love you, too, Logan. You're the only best friend I've ever had."

She threw herself into his arms. He felt utter disappointment. She loved him. *Like a friend.* He felt like he had been punched in the gut. His confession about his true feelings halted before it could be voiced. "Me, too. I'm sorry, but I've got to head home."

"I'm glad you told me in person, and that I could see you one last time, Logan."

He hugged her. "Me, too. Goodbye, Koty. I'll call you when I get there, okay?"

"You'd better," she replied tearfully.

He held out his hand, and she took it. They walked back to his car in silence.

They embraced a final time. Logan kissed the top of her head. When he looked into her eyes, he was suddenly lost. Whatever hold he was caught up in, it was more than he could shake. Before he knew it, he lowered his head and kissed Dakota on her lips. He felt her stiffen, but she did not pull away and slap him. That was a good sign.

The kiss lengthened in duration, and after a few moments, Logan reluctantly stepped back. Dakota's hand flew to her mouth. Her eyes mirrored her shock.

"Dakota, I... You mean the world to me. I don't want to lose you."

"You won't," she said softly. "Promise me you'll keep in touch."

"I promise, Dakota. Don't worry, I'll be home before you know it."

"You'd better," she choked out.

He glanced at her a final time before sliding behind the wheel and driving off. Logan did not look back. There was no way he could bear the devastated look on her face. Besides, his expression mirrored it perfectly.

Logan gripped the steering wheel until his knuckles were white. The sheer weight of family responsibility rested on his shoulders. He would bear it. He had no choice. The entire ride home, he willed his heart not to break under the pressure of his unrequited love for Dakota.

Dream's over, Montague. She's gone, and you've blown it.

Chapter 1

That old letch should've been grateful that all I dropped over his bald head was a tureen of minestrone. It should have been a brick!

Dakota Carson was still steaming about the previous evening's turn of events. If someone would have told her that her perfect day would end with her pouring a bowl of hot soup on a business colleague and threatening him with bodily harm, she would have thought them insane. But it occurred nonetheless.

Roger Thompson had leveraged their business dinner into a ploy to get her into bed. Dakota accepted the dinner meeting because he had something that she wanted—his connection to Amadeus Rothschild, a new designer who specialized in sheets that were elegant and pleasurable to the touch. The fact that he only used a design once made them unique. Since he was the elusive owner of a company called Sheet Music in New England, Dakota had no doubt that he would soon be a household name. The problem was that he only sold his sheets through Roger.

When her client's wife, Nancy Janson, had seen a set on display at Thompson's Textiles, she flipped. She wanted them for her St. Charles, Illinois, bed-and-breakfast, and nothing else would do. Since Roger was local, and Dakota had a good relationship with him, they discussed it over dinner. He promised to supply them for her project, but soon it became evident why an evening appointment was better suited for their discussion. The moment his intentions were clear, she turned him down flat. When Roger refused to take no for an answer, Dakota left money to cover her portion of the bill and bid him good-night. When she walked past him, Roger's arm ensnared her like a vise grip. His mistake.

"Release me," she had demanded.

"Wait, Dakota. Don't leave yet. We can come to an arrangement that will benefit both of us. I have what you want, and you have something I want." Roger had tried to reel her in.

"I don't think so," she had countered smoothly. "In fact, you either remove your hand from my arm right now, or I'll rip that toupee off your head, and then stomp on it like a Flamenco dancer."

He'd complied immediately, but continued to proposition her. That did it. Dakota's answer to his vile suggestions was to pour soup on his head. Roger's toupee cascaded off his dome, along with the soup. She'd chuckled. It had been a sight to see.

"We're done, Roger. Step through my office door again, and you'll regret it."

Her alarm blared into the silence. Stunned at the offending noise that ricocheted off the walls, Dakota almost bolted from her bed. The memory of Roger and his tumbling hairpiece was pushed aside. She had bigger problems.

Last night had caused a hiccup in her plans. Roger's store was a good source of upscale home goods, and he had lots of connections. Now she needed a plan B, and her colleague was now regaled to the Trouser Snake category of people that Dakota had severed all ties with. She knew he would never give up Rothschild's contact information. She was desperate to make her client happy, but was not about to play games, or to sleep her way into opportunities. She took her career very seriously, and if somebody didn't like it, that was their misfortune. That went for the few men she had dated, too.

When Dakota turned on her cell phone, her voice mail icon, email and text message notifications all dinged, buzzed and chirped respectively. Three were from Norma Jean Anderson.

"Now I know you can't possibly be so busy that you can't return my phone calls," Norma Jean said in one message. "It's obvious that you're avoiding m—"

Delete. Dakota felt no shame.

"Dakota Carson, I know your grandmother didn't raise you to—"

Delete. Again.

"Girl, if you don't call me, I'm coming to see you."

She pondered that one, then pressed delete.

Norma Jean and her husband, Heathcliffe, lived a few doors down from her grandparents' house in Chicago. Since the age of thirteen, Dakota considered Norma Jean the neighborhood mom. The woman knew everyone's name, brought homemade meals when people were sick and wouldn't hesitate to give a neighbor whatever she had. Norma Jean had become her rock when she desperately needed someone in her corner, and for that Dakota owed her a lifetime of gratitude. Norma Jean Anderson was an amazing humanitarian. *But a horrible matchmaker.*

Dakota loved Norma Jean, affectionately called Ms. Jeannie, to death, and would do anything for her, but the woman was driving her insane. She was more focused on Dakota's love life than Dakota was, and had been for years. Personal relationships did not work out for Dakota. An occasional date was one thing, but she wasn't getting serious—with anyone. She learned the hard way long ago that men came and went, but work was constant. She had governed her life by that simple observation, and she wasn't about to change now.

Logan and his cousin, Adrian Anderson, sat in his aunt's kitchen eating the most delicious cinnamon roll he had ever tasted. He took a sip of coffee. "Aunt Jeannie," he said slowly. "I appreciate everything you do for me, but I'm not going out with your bowling mate's sister's niece—no matter how many times you ask. Adrian already warned me about her, and as much as I love you, I'm not taking the bait."

Indignant, Norma Jean let out a frustrated breath and pinned her son, Adrian, with a withering look. "This is all *your* fault."

"Oh, no, you don't," Adrian replied between bites of his breakfast. "*You* are the one who doesn't know when to leave well enough alone. I told you two weeks ago that Logan wasn't interested in being set up. Apparently, you turned down your hearing aid."

"I don't wear a hearing aid," she snapped.

"Well, then you played deaf, because you didn't listen. He's been back in town three days, Mom. Let him get acclimated first before you whip out the little black book—or your love-broker encyclopedia."

"Watch it," she replied. Getting up from the table, she started clearing away the dishes. She tried to grab Logan's, but he batted her hand away. "Well, this is a pickle. It's already been arranged."

Logan regarded her with determined purpose. "Then unarrange it. Aunt Jeannie, I haven't even unpacked all my boxes yet, so I definitely don't have time to date. There's no way I'm wasting two hours of my evening trying to make small talk with a woman I've never met, and that I'm not remotely attracted to."

"How do you—" Norma Jean stopped and cut her eyes over to Adrian. "You showed him her picture?"

A wide grin shot across his face. "Yep."

"Adrian," she chided. "Logan deserves happiness, too. Milán is an incredible woman, and an even better daughter-in-law. She'll make a wonderful mother, too. That is, whenever you get around to—"

"We're not having this conversation again," Adrian interrupted.

"We wouldn't have to if you'd made good on the promise of giving me grandbabies."

"Mom, it's been two years, not ten. Cut us some slack. We're practicing as much as we can."

Logan burst out laughing, and patted his cousin on the back.

Norma Jean rolled her eyes. "Do I look amused?"

"Aunt Jeannie, it may not seem like it, but I'm perfectly capable of finding my own dates."

"You don't say? Is that why you're still single?"

"I haven't found the right girl yet," he countered.

"Hmph. Seems to me you *had* the possibility of the right girl, but you let her go."

His expression darkened. Like he needed a reminder of his ruined relationship with Dakota, or the tense circumstances surrounding why he had left in the first place. Finishing the last of his meal, Logan stood up and put his plate in the dishwasher. "As much as I love these family get-togethers, and reminiscing about subjects I'd prefer not to talk about, I really have to get going. I'm leaving for Jamaica tomorrow."

Norma Jean frowned. "How long will you be gone?"

"Just a few days."

"Have you seen Dakota yet?"

"No. At some point I plan to, but I'm not sure how well that'll go."

"Tread lightly," Norma Jean cautioned. "Time has a way of changing folks. Life happens, Logan. She's not the same girl you left behind years ago."

He looked at her. "What does that mean?"

Norma Jean shrugged her shoulders. "I'm just saying… things change…people change."

"Look, I know you mean well, but as far as renewing my friendship with Dakota…I don't even know if that's possible. The last few times I've been back haven't gone so well."

"What did you expect? You haven't exactly leveled with her, Logan."

"Aunt Jeannie, I know your heart's in the right place, but can you just let it go? Right now the water is still, and I'd like to keep it that way." He kissed Norma Jean's cheek. "Thanks for breakfast. It was…interesting."

Norma Jean handed him a plastic container with more cinnamon rolls. "Anytime, sweetie." She returned the kiss and tapped him on the chest with her index finger. "We're not done talking yet. Remember what I said, and there's always time to right a wrong, Logan. You and Dakota were the best of friends and I—"

Logan headed out of the kitchen. "You're beating a dead horse that ain't coming alive."

Adrian kissed his mother and then fell into step beside his cousin. "At least you didn't get fixed up with one."

"I heard that," his mother called out from behind them.

Logan and Adrian continued to laugh and compare notes as they walked out.

Retrieving his car keys from his pocket, Logan glanced at him. "Well, that was brutal. Remind me again how I got on her radar? I've only been back three days."

"Quit complaining. That was two days longer than my friends and I wagered on. I lost fifty bucks on you. Though I may still have a chance. The second bet is that you'll be off the market by Christmas. Which, by the way, is just three months away."

"Save your money. I have no intention of being caught up in Aunt Jeannie's machinations."

Adrian aimed the remote at his vehicle. "Yeah, that's what we all said."

Logan got in and started his car. He glanced at his phone. The ringer was turned down. He had missed several calls, one of them from his mother. *There was no way Aunt Jeannie could have called her that fast.* Turning the engine off, he decided to get it over with.

"Hey, Mom," he said when she picked up. "How are you?"

"I'm fine, honey," Beverly Montague replied with excitement. "How's Chicago? Are you settling in okay?"

"Yep. The condo is fine. I'm still unpacking, but I should be done by the weekend."

"I'm glad."

"How are things going without Dad? Are you lonely?"

"No, indeed," she said quickly. "Don't get me wrong. I love and miss my husband, but your father and Heathcliffe are having a ball fishing. I get daily…sometimes more often…reports on what they're up to." She laughed. "It's great to hear them sounding like a bunch of young guys out on a weekend pass."

Logan chuckled. "Considering it's Dad we're talking about, that's shocking. He's not exactly the sit-back-and-relax type of guy."

"You'd be surprised. Ever since you took over at Belle Cove, he's only had to focus on running Montague International. He's got a solid executive team in place, so he's been learning to slow down. Personally, I think retirement is the best thing for him, but I know he'll never let go one hundred percent. Still, your taking over the resorts has been a tremendous help, honey. I know it wasn't easy, but you have exceeded our expectations. You've fit in wonderfully, and made solid contributions to the company since you started. I'm so proud of you, Logan. We both are."

He felt a surge of gratification. "Thanks, Mom. That means a lot to me. So what are you doing while they're gone?" he said, changing the subject. "Something tells me you're not at home crocheting."

"Heavens, no," Beverly said quickly. "The ladies and I have been having a fun time with our charity projects... and a few excursions."

The way she said it tipped Logan off that his mother was indeed making good use of his father's being away. He was not worried, though—his parents loved each other and had for over thirty-five years. As for his aunt and uncle, they were the most solid couple he knew, next to his parents.

"Do I even want to know the details?" he joked.

"Uh, no. That way, if your dad asks you for the particulars, you can answer him honestly."

Logan let out a robust laugh. "Gotcha."

"Enough about me. What's this I hear about you blowing off a date your aunt set up for you?"

The smile slid right off his face. Apparently, Aunt Jeannie *had* made the rounds. His mother had heard about the potential date and promptly sided with her sister-in-law. Normally, his uncle Heathcliffe would temper his aunt's plotting, but since he and his father were silver-salmon fishing in Alaska, he was on his own.

"Mom, now isn't the best time to worry about my love life. I'm in the middle of some transitional things at Belle Cove, and that has to be my primary focus."

In addition to the corporation, the Montagues owned three resorts in Ocho Rios, Jamaica, Sanibel Island, Florida, and St. Simon's Island, Georgia. When he took over as CEO of the resorts months before, Logan's focus was to increase their bottom line, and to position the business for the future to ensure that Belle Resorts stayed competitive. Eventually, Logan realized that to accomplish the goals he had set for himself and the company, he would need to take a different approach. He would need to go outside the confines of the company to get the expertise needed in order to successfully effect a change.

"Are you listening to me?"

"Huh?" Logan realized he'd missed something his mother had said. "I'm sorry, Mom, what did you say?"

"I said, I know you're finding your way at Montague, but try not to lose sight of the things in life that really matter, honey. Work is constant, and God willing, will always be there. Your personal life can pass you by in the blink of an eye if you're not careful."

"Well, that's an about-face. I seem to recall years ago you both saying that there was nothing more important than business, and it was my personal life that had to take a backseat."

"Logan, that's the way it had to be at that time. I know you still blame us for what happened with Dakota, and I'm truly sorry for that. I just assumed that you'd be able to fix everything when you came home."

"That's not how it worked out, is it?" Logan said bitterly.

"No. No, it's not. And your father and I are saddened by it, but at that time, Logan, it was extremely important for you to learn the family business. That was the priority then, but it doesn't have to be now. You'll find happiness, sweetheart. I know it. Which is why you should give Jeannie a chance to—"

"Not happening, Mom. Now isn't the time for me to be navigating Aunt Jeannie's blind-date circuit. I've still got a lot of work to do."

"Okay, but you need to find a balance between the two," she warned. "Oh, Jeannie also mentioned you'd hired Dakota to give the place a facelift. How's she doing? I heard her new company is doing well, and that she's sure to be a big help revitalizing Belle Cove. I can't wait to see the finished product. I really miss her. It's a shame you two weren't able to reconnect over the years, but maybe now you'll be able to catch up."

"I haven't hired her yet. I'm planning to discuss it with her soon. Hey, I've got to run, but I'll call you later. I love you."

"Love you, too, Logan. And don't think I don't know a redirect when I see one," she said sweetly.

He hung up the phone and leaned back in his seat. Logan was not good at admitting that he needed help of any kind, but there was more at stake here than just his pride. That was battered and bruised enough, thanks to the choices he had made over the years. Still, coming back to Chicago after such a long absence was bittersweet. It was great being in close proximity to his family again, but that wasn't the main reason he decided to come back.

One thing prompted his relocation, and he could no longer ignore the all-consuming influence it held over him: rectifying the mistake he had made years ago—losing Dakota Carson. He loved her. Still. He had tried considerably over the years to get over her, and to move on, but all his relationships had failed miserably. To him, it felt as though he were constantly trying to shove a square peg into a round hole. It just was not going to happen. He needed to rework his destiny and win her back. When he left, they were on the cusp of something, and he was convinced that they needed to explore the possibilities. Logan was confident that in time, he could achieve his heart's desire, and he did not need his aunt's help to do it.

Chapter 2

"You sound like a hot mess," Susan said.

"Thanks," Dakota replied. "I didn't sleep very well. What's up?"

"Mrs. Anderson called—again," her best friend and office manager, Susan Summers, replied. "She wants you to call back ASAP."

"It's eight in the morning."

"She said it was important."

"I'll bet she did," Dakota groused. "I'll call her shortly."

"Okay, but she said she had some information for you that was pretty important."

"I'm not really in the mood to speak with anyone right now."

"Why?"

She sighed. "It's a long, bizarre story about designer sheets, soup and toupees. I'll fill you in on the way to work."

"I can't wait to hear the details."

Dakota hung up and went back to her laptop. She checked her schedule. There was only one meeting for the day. *That's hardly going to get you into the black ink.*

Her business had been open less than six months. She had several clients, but her customers did not need her on a regular basis. One Eighty Renovations specialized in taking businesses that suffered from outdated decor, branding and staffing woes and turning them back into a hot commodity. Dakota took a holistic approach to re-energize her client's consumer appeal, from the CEO's attire, to the office chairs and the plates on the table at a luncheon meeting. When it came to improving the corporate image, nothing was off-limits.

Right now you need to improve your *image...your financial image.*

Since college, Dakota realized the value of self-reliance. She did not need anyone guiding her path. Not relying on others meant never being disappointed. Failure would be at her own hands, and that was not an option. A wave of melancholia swept over her. She closed her eyes and allowed herself to get swept back to a time when life was simple...easier. Her mother's warm smile, the sage advice of her father and the one man she thought she would have in her life forever. *Logan.* With a heavy heart, Dakota forced herself back to the present.

She shut her laptop. Why was his aunt trying to reach her, and what was so dire? *Probably another sermon on how I need to settle down and find Mr. Right.*

"Well, that's never gonna happen because there's no such thing as Mr. Right." *If anything, it was more like Mr. Right Now.*

Two hours later, she stepped into the elevator at work. The small office space she rented on South LaSalle Street in Chicago's Loop district was the perfect place to grow a business, and near all the major transit lines. It had an art-deco feel with tall, white semigloss walls and tray ceilings. The bright decor contrasted nicely with the rich, cherry wood trim and the dark gray and burgundy textured carpet. There was a conference room, two large offices, a kitchen and reception area. The bathroom was just outside her suite. She loved the compact space. It was elegant, and the accessories and artwork she had chosen complemented the leather furniture. When she opened the glass door to her suite and walked in, a sense of pride practically overwhelmed her. One Eighty Renovations was her life's blood she had built from whole cloth. She vowed it would flourish.

Susan was in the process of taking a bite out of her bagel when Dakota walked in.

"Well, if it isn't the sex toy."

Dakota snorted. "Don't even get me started. Thanks to the Casanova of Home Goods, I need another path to Amadeus Rothschild—and fast."

"Let me get this straight—you get propositioned by one of your suppliers, and all you're worried about are the designer linens?"

"Yes. I've got a problem to solve, and I'm going to solve it. Dig up whatever you can on Mr. Rothschild and his company, Sheet Music. Someone we know besides Roger has to have his phone number. Call in some favors, make some promises…do whatever it takes to find him."

"Sure thing. What about Mr. Thompson?"

"Forget him. I'm not some conquest, or here to appease his ego. I've dealt with the situation. Time to focus on landing a new client."

"Sounds great. Got any ideas?"

"A few. Follow me."

Susan got up and headed into Dakota's office. She took a seat in the chair across from Dakota's desk with her computer tablet in hand. "I'm all ears. Impress me."

"She's been doing that to me for years." A man's voice sounded behind them.

Both women looked up in unison. Dakota's eyes flew

to the doorway. The color drained off her face. She stood up shakily and braced her desk.

"Dakota, are you okay?" Susan whispered.

"Logan."

"Hello, Koty."

"Koty?" Susan's eyebrow rose. "I thought you hated that nickname?"

Dakota glanced at Logan. Despite the shock at seeing him, she schooled her features. When she spoke, her voice was firm. "No, just the person who used to use it."

Logan crossed the room at an unhurried pace. "Is that how you greet a long-lost friend?"

"You were hardly lost," she clarified. "You left, if I recall."

"Well, that part may be true."

"May be?" Dakota retorted. "You destroyed our friendship, Logan. You left abruptly—and you didn't look back." She left out the part about when she needed him most.

Susan glanced between the two of them. "Uh, I think I'll let you two catch up."

She stood up and bolted from the room.

The lofty reply got under Dakota's skin in record time and spurred her to action. She was across the room in seconds.

"What are you doing here?"

Logan sat down on the couch. "Are you going to stand here hissing at me like an angry kitten, or are you going to welcome a good friend home?"

"There's that word again," she replied. "I haven't seen you in how many years, Logan? I'd hardly call us friends—good or otherwise."

"We were inseparable once."

"Yes, we were…and then you ruined it."

He nodded. "Fair enough, but it's not like I've changed much, Koty."

"Nope, still the selfish jackass you've always been," she quipped. "And it's Dakota. Nobody calls me Koty… not anymore."

"How about we call a cease-fire, and you ask me why I'm here?"

"How about you explain why you stayed away in the first place? Better yet, why you didn't level with me if your feelings had changed, and why you're sitting here like I'm supposed to run into your arms and give you a big welcome-home hug. I can tell you right now, that ain't happening."

"Can you please sit down and let me explain?"

With an exasperated sigh, Dakota took a seat across from him. "I'm sitting. Now why are you here? I thought Chicago was the last place you wanted to be?"

He winced at the not-so-subtle reminder of words spoken long ago that she had overheard. "For a long time it was…but things change."

Her expression was guarded. "I know that better than anyone."

He sighed. "I did come back, often, if I recall."

"Yes, you did, but nothing was ever the same. Tell me I'm wrong. Each time I saw you things were…awkward between us."

"I don't expect you to understand, but I stayed away to make a name for myself."

"Last time I checked, you were a Montague. How many names do you need?"

"You know what I mean. I left at my father's insistence to learn the family business, but I also went in search of life on my own terms…without all the baggage—and the money. It was important to me."

"Obviously more important than our friendship."

His expression turned remorseful. "You know that wasn't the case."

"Do I?" She stared at him. "What was I supposed to think, Logan? You spouted some gibberish about going off to work at Montague…something you said you'd never do."

"It was at my parents' insistence, Dakota. I didn't exactly have a choice in the matter. I never *wanted* to leave Chicago—or you."

"But you kissed me…we kissed, Logan. You literally ask me to wait for you, and then you leave and go to New York, but that's not the best part. Then you go to California to attend Stanford instead of Georgetown University like we planned. You didn't tell me about your decision until it was too late to stop you. Which I'm sure you bargained for."

Logan glanced up. "Dakota, nothing during those years turned out the way I'd hoped. It was wrong of me to ask you to put your life on hold for me, but…I thought we had something developing between us that we should explore."

"So did I, but then things changed."

"I know. I'm sorry, Dakota."

When she remained quiet, he continued. "So you did end up going to Georgetown?"

"That was the plan," she said pointedly. "I kept my end of our promise. And to add insult to injury, you didn't keep in contact."

The bitter censure in her words was not lost on Logan.

"So what about you?"

She looked confused. "What about me?"

"You didn't bother to visit. You knew where I was, and you didn't come. Not once."

"Are you kidding, I—"

Dakota clamped her mouth shut. She was about to confess that she had come to visit, but stopped before she could humiliate herself by telling him the truth. She would never admit that she did go to see him, but that when she reached his dorm room and a friend let her in, she discovered Logan in bed with another woman. That's when her heart had shattered into a heap at her feet, and she realized that she had loved Logan—and lost him. She swore he would never know the extent of her pain, or heartbreak. That one kiss they shared before he left was their first… and last.

"You what?"

"Nothing," she said quickly. "You're right. I'm the bad guy here."

"I never said that."

"I didn't come see you when I could have. Truth is, I found myself very unmotivated to travel across the country to see a man who didn't want to be in the same city with me."

It bothered her, being so affected by their busted-up friendship. It should have been water under the bridge—too many things had occurred since he left. He was absent when she needed him most. To see him now after so many years of silence was like a well-placed chisel chipping away at a wall of ice.

"It wasn't that, Dakota. I…wanted to see you. I never stopped wanting to see you."

"Yeah? Well, your actions spoke way louder than words, Logan."

He leaned forward, resting his elbows on his legs. "Koty, I know that I hurt you…terribly, and that I can never fix what I…threw away. And I get that you don't want to see me, but I'm here to make things right between us."

"How do you propose to do that, Logan?" she scoffed. "A time machine?"

"I'd use it if I had one. Since I don't, I need you to hear me out. I've got an idea that could be advantageous—to both of us."

Dakota crossed her arms in front of her. If she was going to be fed a line, she wanted to be good and comfortable. "Fine, Logan, let's hear it."

"I want to hire you to renovate my resorts."

"*Your* resorts? I thought your parents were still at the helm."

He shook his head. "They stepped down a few months ago and put me in charge. Dad still runs Montague, but I'm the new CEO of Belle Resorts."

"Great for you, but why do you want me?"

"You're the only one I've ever wanted."

Her eyebrow arched upward. "You could've fooled me."

"For this job," he explained. "Your caliber of expertise is just what Belle Cove needs to introduce her to a whole new demographic. She has to change with the times, Dakota. Right now we're viewed as too elitist, and unapproachable. If we're to prosper, we need more overall appeal. While still remaining luxurious, of course."

She shook her head. "I can't believe you want me to work for you."

"I do, but more important, given our history…*can* you work for me?"

Dakota pondered all the ramifications to herself and her business. It was a no-brainer. Business trumped heart, every time. Dakota's gaze connected with his. "Yes."

Relief suffused his face. Logan stood up. "I'm glad to hear that. I thought you'd throw me out on my ear."

"I considered it."

Logan headed to the door, and Dakota followed.

"I just want you to know that I believe that eventually, we can get past our differences."

Dakota looked skeptical. "Only time will tell."

* * *

Later that evening, Logan was at his condo going over his discussion with Dakota. Their initial meeting after years of silence had not gone exactly to plan. Somehow, he thought that time would have mellowed both of them, but he was wrong. Dead wrong. Surprisingly, Dakota was still angry at him. It was true that he had severed all ties unexpectedly and completely, but Logan was not without remorse. He wanted so much more, and leaving her had damn near killed him, but he always held out hope that they could reconnect.

Though they were best friends, Logan had developed feelings for her early on. When she had begun dating, and found her first boyfriend, Logan was upset at his hesitation at declaring those feelings. His jealously had directly resulted in his betraying that friendship—and her.

There were hundreds of times he wanted to confess his part in the breakup with her first boyfriend, Michael, a few months before Logan left, but something always stopped him. His heart had overruled his head and better judgment. It gave him hope that Dakota could return his feelings. It was a small chance, but he had allowed the seed to grow inside his heart. He reasoned that she would be free, and then he would confess his love to her in hopes that they could have a relationship.

In his mind, she would turn to him and reciprocate his love, but that plan went wrong. Horribly and irrevocably wrong. He had not anticipated that Michael would alert Dakota to his part in their breakup. When she found out, there were no words to describe her anger. He also had not factored in his parents stepping in with their family crisis and ruining his perfectly thought-out plan.

Suddenly, it was all too much. His family's expectations for his future, and Dakota's discovery of his role in her unhappiness.

The argument that resulted between them had been bitter. He deserved every angry and hurt-laced word she had hurled at him. When they reconciled, he decided to come clean and tell her the truth about his motivation behind his actions, but then he was forced to leave town. His biggest regret was that he had not been brave enough to level with Dakota, and that she had been collateral damage in his father's quest for bringing him into the family business, and his jealous tampering with her love life. Logan had vowed to tell her the truth, and now was his chance to come clean. About everything.

Time had a way of fostering introspection, and sitting there earlier staring at Dakota's rigid, angry, gorgeous face was making him ponder his ability to remain quiet. And sane. It was like a glimpse back in time. In many ways she was the eighteen-year-old girl he had left, but she was different, too. She had matured, and grown into her beauty. She was taller, shapelier, and her skin was still flawless, except for the dark circles under her eyes that she had attempted to hide with concealer. Though these eyes were bright with challenge, Logan could still see the underlying pain in them when she looked at him.

Because of you.

A knot of regret blossomed in Logan's stomach. He assumed that only he would carry the loss of their relationship, and that she would forget him and immerse herself in other friends and school. Logan wagered that only his heart would be sacrificed.

You were wrong.

That realization hit Logan squarely in his gut. He wasn't blind. Dakota had done more than suffer at his desertion. There was a sadness about her that he had not anticipated. She was still troubled. She deserved much better than that—than him. But God help him, he refused to give up the minuscule hope that he could make amends. The one kiss they shared still resided in his memories and taunted him with the realization of lost dreams. Whatever it took, Logan would earn her forgiveness, and eventually her heart. It was a herculean task, but the prize was a lifetime of happiness spent with the only woman in the world whom he had ever loved.

Chapter 3

*W*hoever wrote *be careful what you ask for, you may get it*, obviously knew what the heck they were talking about. "I vow to do anything to keep my business afloat, and *bam!* In walks Logan Montague." Dakota laughed at the irony, but it came out as more of a high-pitched squeak. *What kind of sick joke is that?*

"Daydreaming again?"

Dakota was leaning so far back in her chair that it almost capsized. She had to put forth a lot of effort to right herself.

"I did knock," Susan said. "And I called your name."

"I'm starting to think that I need a bell over my door," Dakota said, panting from exertion.

Susan sat down, took a sip of coffee from her mug and got comfortable. "So how did it go yesterday? Did you catch up with your friend?"

"Not exactly."

"I didn't press you yesterday because I could see you were overwhelmed, but...I can't believe you didn't tell me about Logan. I'm your best friend. Don't you think I should've known about something this important to you?"

"What was I supposed to say?"

"How about the truth?"

With a long sigh, Dakota fiddled with a paper clip. "We

were the best of friends, he moved away to go learn the family business, which he said he'd never do, and then he stayed away to make a name for himself outside of his wealthy parents' shadow, and now he's back."

"And?"

Dakota shrugged. "And I'm fine."

A skeptical expression flittered across Susan's face. "Your body language says otherwise."

"Look, I know you're concerned about me, but you don't have to be. I can take care of myself," Dakota assured her friend. "I have been for quite some time."

"I know you have," Susan said softly. "You've endured more than anyone should, and I don't doubt your voracity when it comes to watching your own back. But it's obvious there's more to this story than you're telling. I saw it in your eyes the moment he walked in."

"Saw what?"

"It wasn't just surprise at seeing a long-lost friend. There was more—and it had nothing to do with friendship."

She sat forward. "Suzy, I love you…you know that, but I don't want to talk about it. Besides, I've got important news. Our new client is Belle Resorts."

"Wow. Their resorts are so beautiful. It's a fitting name."

"It is. Logan's mom visited the area while on vacation and—"

Susan's mouth dropped open. "Wait a minute…are you telling me that your friend's family owns them?"

"Yes. It's a family business, and Logan is the new CEO."

"Seriously? I know about the one in Jamaica, but how many are there?"

Dakota studied her desk. "Not many."

"Dakota," Susan pressed.

"There's only…three."

Susan choked on her coffee. "Three? Are you kidding? We don't have the manpower to—"

"I know, but we'll start with the one in Jamaica first, and if that goes well, One Eighty will tackle the rest, one at a time." Dakota leaned across her desk. "This is a great opportunity," she said excitedly.

"I know, but are you sure you can handle it?"

"Of course we can."

"Not *we*," Susan corrected. "You."

"Yes. We've been talking about expanding, right?"

"I'm not completely sold on this idea. It's obvious that you and Mr. CEO have a few…issues to work out."

"Yes, we do, but we can tackle those later. Logan assured me that he had no problems taking direction from me, and I made it clear that if we do this, I want complete autonomy. No exceptions."

"And he agreed to that."

"Yes. I gave him a contract, and Logan will have it couriered over when it's ready."

"If you think you can handle it, I'm in one hundred percent."

Dakota jumped up and went to hug her friend. "Thanks, and don't worry. I've got this. Everything will run as smooth as kookoon silk, trust me."

She returned the hug. "I know it will. Speaking of which—" She handed Dakota a piece of paper.

"What's this?"

"The most recent message that Norma Jean Anderson has left today. You'd better stop stalling and call Ms. Jeannie back before she comes looking for you."

"Too late," Norma Jean said from the doorway.

"This is getting to be a habit," Susan joked before greeting the older woman and leaving.

Norma Jean got straight to the point. "I know you've gotten my messages."

"Ms. Jeannie, I promise that I'm not avoiding you. I just got an unexpected new client, and I'm trying to work a few things out."

"Well, there's a development that I think you should know about," Norma Jean began.

"No need. Logan stopped by to see me yesterday."

"He did?" she said, astonished. "Good. I know you two don't have the best history, but I hope you were able to clear the air."

"Not really, but I can handle it," Dakota assured her.

"I know things don't always go according to plan, honey," Norma Jean said. "There's no denying that he messed up really bad, but I know he's here to make things right between you. You were so close once. I'm hoping that you and my nephew can get that back."

"I don't know about that."

"Have you told him what happened years ago?"

A frown creased Dakota's forehead. "No. Did you?"

"It's not my place. It's your life, and if you choose not to tell him what happened after he left, I won't be the one enlightening him. I guess you'll fill Logan in in your own good time."

"I…I'm not sure, Ms. Jeannie. I've been mad at him for so long, I honestly don't know if things will ever be right between us, but we've called a temporary cease-fire for now. I won't lie, a part of me wants to leave well enough alone, and never see him again, but he's making me a business offer that I would be foolish to turn down. Besides, I don't have time for a bruised heart."

Norma Jean shook her head with displeasure. "It's more than bruised, Dakota. You experienced a devastating event in your life. It's completely understandable how it would alter how you view things, but you defer your personal life too much if you ask me. You need to get your house in order."

Dakota was still mulling over Norma Jean's words on the drive home. Norma Jean was a wonderful woman, but when she got a notion in her head, nothing was going to deter her from her goal. As far as Dakota was concerned, she had given love a shot, and got kicked in the teeth. She was happy, and then everything got stripped away. Dakota accepted that sometimes as much as you want something, there's no guarantee that it's meant to be.

It was late by the time she left work, so she stopped at one of her favorite Mediterranean restaurants to pick up dinner. Dakota lived less than twenty miles from Chicago in the suburban village of Glenview. When she got home, she took a quick shower and changed into loungewear. She ate dinner while searching Belle Resort's company website. Jotting down notes on a pad as she went, Dakota focused on first impressions and action items that she would organize later.

She clicked another link and discovered a travel magazine article on Logan's taking over the resorts. It was a good article, but the writer pondered whether Logan had enough experience working in the hospitality industry and if it would ultimately hurt the family's resort chain. Apparently, bookings had dropped when the transition was announced, but had slowly edged their way back. She stared at Logan's picture. He was wearing a navy blue suit with a bold red-striped silk tie. There was a slight tan to his golden-brown skin, and he had a smile that made him appear confident and capable. He also looked as though he held a secret.

He also looked incredibly good.

Dakota stared at her laptop screen. There was no denying that Logan was good-looking. He had classic features, and at six-foot-two, he was well-built and muscular. Inheriting his mother's sable-brown eyes, he also had her knack for winning people over. When he smiled, his whole face lit up, which only served to make him much more irresistible. What bothered Dakota is why her conscience had just reminded her of that fact.

There were no disillusions at having to work with Logan. It would be a huge test of her patience and fortitude because she still wanted to wring his neck sometimes, but violent thoughts notwithstanding, Dakota was excited to be working on a new project, especially one with the potential for add-on work later.

Her phone rang, interrupting her musings.

"Hey, Koty."

She frowned. "Having second thoughts?"

"About you?" He chuckled. "Never. I believe you're the perfect woman for the job," Logan assured her.

She relaxed. "Why?"

"Your company has received a great deal of accolades in the short time you've been in business. You know your stuff, and your vision to date has never been wrong."

Unable to help herself, she felt her chest swell with pride. "How do you know?"

"I read and asked around."

That did not surprise her, and yet it did.

"I didn't need validation that you're good, if that's what you're thinking."

A smile crept up her face. "I was thinking no such thing."

"Liar. I've got decisive plans for Belle Cove. I need you to transform my vision into something tangible...that will seduce our guests. What I need to know is can you do that, Koty?"

Could she do that? Heck yeah, she could.

"I'm confident that I can give you exactly what your company needs."

"Great, then how about we meet tomorrow to discuss it further?"

Dakota agreed, and then hung up. She went back to her spot at the table and resumed her work on finding everything she could get her hands on pertaining to Belle Resorts…and Logan.

It was still dark outside when Dakota arrived early to work the next morning. She had gotten hardly any sleep, but that was of little consequence. The preliminary ideas rolling around in her head were now down on paper. She felt good about them, but would need to garner input from Logan. She would also need to schedule an on-site inspection as soon as possible so that she could spend some time evaluating their business practices and operations from the ground up. That was when Dakota really got in and rolled up her sleeves. Her presence unnerved people at times, but it was imperative to her job.

Logan had arrived at nine, and stayed over two hours while he presented his briefing to Dakota. When he was done, she had a better understanding of where he wanted to lead the company.

"So, how soon can you make yourself available to go down and check things out?"

"Immediately," she replied.

"Great. How about Friday?"

Dakota nodded. "That's fine."

"How long do you think you'll need for your evaluation?"

"Normally it takes a few days to conduct interviews, do an inspection and tour the facility on my own. I'd like to interact with the guests, as well. You know, ask some questions and get their impressions. From there I'll together a design briefing on the proposed changes."

They finalized arrangements before Logan stood up to leave.

"I'll have my travel agent contact you immediately."

"That'll be fine."

"Great. I'll see you Friday. I'm looking forward to your visit."

"Me, too."

No sooner had Logan left than Susan came into Dakota's office.

"That went well."

"It sure did," Dakota said with a smile.

"I stand corrected. Apparently, you will be able to handle working with Logan."

"Told you. By the way, I'll be going to Jamaica on Friday."

Susan sighed. "Warm breezes, breathtaking views, sun and pristine sand. Oh, I wish I were going. It's about time I had another island fling."

"Another?" Dakota laughed. "You mean the first one, don't you?"

Susan leaned back in her chair. "A girl can dream, can't she? Jamaica is a wonderful place to kindle a romance." Her gaze rested on Dakota. "Or rekindle one."

Dakota blushed. "I wouldn't know. Logan and I only kissed once. We never had a romance, so there's no fire to stoke."

Her friend's gaze missed nothing. "But you wanted one."

* * *

Adrian dug his hand into the bowl of Hunter Mix. He chewed softly and then washed it down with a swig of his beer. "So, how's your Win Dakota Back plan going?"

Logan put his feet up on his coffee table and regarded his cousin. "It's a bit early for status updates, isn't it?"

Adrian shrugged. "Maybe. Maybe not. Things could be progressing at an alarming pace for all I know."

"Nope, but then I knew that going in. I'm not putting time limits on anything. Dakota and I have a lot of ground to cover."

"Don't I know it," Adrian said with a wry smile. "You should've seen how long it took Milán and me to declare a truce, but when we did…"

Logan held up a hand. "Spare me the details."

"It's not what you think. We were friends quite a while before anything turned serious."

"Yeah, well, Dakota and I aren't even that. She is amicable toward me, but that's strictly for work purposes."

"Are you sure?"

"Of course I am. She's only tolerating being in the same room with me because of the resort. Trust me, I'm under no illusions on that score."

"I'm no stranger to work being the only tie that binds, believe me. I'm not going to lie, you do have your work cut out for you, but she'll come around."

Logan grabbed a handful of nuts. "Hope springs eternal."

"Speaking of eternal, has my mother been pressing you to wade out into the dating pool?"

"Constantly, but I remain immune."

Adrian shook his head. "I love my mother dearly, but sometimes her idea of boundaries is comical."

"I'm seeing that, but don't worry about me. I'll be in

Jamaica with Dakota for the next few days, so I'll be off the radar."

"Logan, you could be in the Antarctic, and you'd still be on Norma Jean's radar."

He laughed at that. "True." He was silent for a few moments but then had to ask, "So, has Dakota been dating anyone?"

"Not that I know of. Why else would my mother be trying so hard to fix her up?"

That bit of news did not sit well with Logan. Up until that point, he had assumed that the only love life Norma Jean was interested in was his. "Has she been successful?"

"About as successful as she's been getting you to go on a date."

Dakota being romantically involved with another man was not on the list of things he enjoyed thinking about. A few times over the years, he had returned to find her in a relationship. Logan had been cordial, but it bothered him. Considering that he was the one who bolted, he knew it was hypocritical to be troubled by it, but his heart did not always agree with his head—especially where she was concerned.

Adrian waved his hand in front of his cousin's face a few times. "Dude, how long are you going to sit here daydreaming about her?"

"What? Sorry, didn't hear you," Logan replied, but what he wanted to say was, as long as it takes.

Chapter 4

What am I going to do about Logan?

By Thursday, Dakota was exhausted for two reasons. The first was that she had worked late every night on her St. Charles project. There was still no luck finding the sought-after Rothschild sheets, and so far Susan's sources yielded no results. She had tried to steer Nancy's tastes in another direction, but her client wasn't having it.

"Darling, did you hear? Bootsie Ellerby has a set of Rothschilds!"

This was not what Dakota wanted to hear. "Really?"

"Yes! It's true! I saw them for myself. My manicurist knows her manicurist, and she told me that Bootsie actually went to Rothschild's home and refused to leave until he agreed to sell her a set. Can you believe it?" Nancy exclaimed. "Apparently, he's loaded. Comes from old, old money. Why he's designing sheets is anyone's guess. Maybe it's some type of hobby. I don't care what it is, I just want those sheets. Bootsie's set was gorgeous. Much nicer than the one I saw at Roger's store. I hope you weren't planning on getting them from him. I think you'd do better going to the source, don't you?

"Wouldn't you know, Bootsie had the gall to refuse to give me his address? She just wants to lord them over me, but we'll show her, won't we, Dakota? I'm sure with your contacts, you've got him on speed dial."

I wish. Relieved that Nancy had come up for air, she wrote down what information she could gather from her client's monologue so that Susan could pursue the lead. Dakota reasoned that Bootsie loved to talk as much as Nancy did, and if that was the case, it was time to get a manicure.

After seeing her client to the door, Dakota left a note for Susan to stop in when she returned from lunch. Needing a break from sheets and Bootsie Ellerby, she focused on Belle Cove—and Logan.

It was not her intention to pique her friend's interest to know more about the past, but as far as Dakota was concerned, their history was ancient.

Still, things had progressed better than she expected. Their last meeting had gone very well. Pictures were great, but Dakota was looking forward to seeing the resort first-hand. She had received a call from his travel agent with instructions for their trip. A car was coming to pick her up and take her to the airport. From there, she would fly to Ocho Rios on the Montagues' company jet. Dakota could not contain the thrill she felt. It would be her first time on a private plane, and she looked forward to the experience.

Dakota's doorbell chimed. *Susan.* Her friend had agreed to help her pack for her trip. When she opened the door, she greeted her bag-laden office manager with a smile.

"You're late. I'm just about finished with the packing."

"Sorry, but now we have more time to socialize."

Dakota shook her head, but stood aside to let Susan enter. "What's all this?"

"I'm sorry I'm late, but I figured with all the packing and worrying you'd be doing, you wouldn't have time to make yourself dinner, so I brought it with me."

She followed Susan to the kitchen and helped her un-
load the cartons of Chinese food.

"I'm not worrying."

"Uh-huh." Susan moved around Dakota's kitchen with
ease. She retrieved two wineglasses and a corkscrew out
of the cabinet while Dakota set the table.

"Thanks for this," she said after Susan poured the wine.

"You're welcome."

"So, are you ready to begin this project?"

Dakota was thoughtful while she chewed. "As ready
as I'll ever be. Who knew after all these years that I'd see
Logan again, much less have him for a client."

"I'll admit, the timing is…interesting," Susan replied.

Dakota let out an unladylike snort. "Don't read too
much into it. I wrote him off once before…and after this
is over, I'll do it again."

"You think it'll be that easy this time?"

"Sure, why not?"

"Why not? Dakota, it's obvious that the two of you have
unfinished business. I'll hand it to you, up until this point,
you've done a very good job of acting like he doesn't exist.
The fact that I didn't know about him, or how deep the history runs between you two, is proof enough."

There was a light hint of censure in Susan's voice that
Dakota did not miss.

"I know. I'm sorry, Suzy. I just… It was hard enough
living through that time in my life without having to relay
what happened to anyone else."

"What *did* happen, Dakota?"

She sighed and sat back in her chair, absentmindedly
swirling the wine in her glass. "It all started with an argument. From the moment I began spending summers at my
grandparents' house, the neighborhood kids made fun of
me for being the outsider. I was getting teased badly by a

group of girls one day, when Logan Montague walked past and heard them. He stood up for me. He was my champion that day. Eventually, we became inseparable, and I spent every summer in Chicago. My parents thought it was better for me to branch out and get to know more kids, but I didn't want to. We played together, spent long hours reading our favorite books, talking about the future, or being knee-deep in some adventure. Logan was my best friend for five years. One day he betrayed me by ruining my relationship with Michael. Not to mention leaving, and breaking my heart—after we kissed, of course."

Susan sat back and crossed her legs to get comfortable. "Whoa, wait. Who's Michael?"

"He was my first boyfriend. Logan didn't like him from the start, and always razzed me about him. He never missed an opportunity to point out how Michael was lacking in some way. I was livid at his interference in my love life, but I was torn because he was my best friend. In the end, I thought him very high-handed to assume Michael wasn't right for me."

"Well, did you talk to him about it?"

"Constantly, but it always ended in arguments, so I ignored his remarks about Michael. I thought I was in love. And *pow,* just like that, it was over. He broke up with me. I was devastated. Later…I found out the extent of Logan's dislike for him."

"How?"

"Michael admitted that he'd been talked into breaking it off with me—by Logan."

Susan gasped. "No way!"

Dakota nodded. "He'd scored courtside seats for a Bulls game, but that didn't stop him from telling me all about Logan's machinations to bust us up. I'm sure Logan didn't factor that into the deal. Sadly, that incident made me realize that in order for Logan's attempts to be successful, it meant Michael wasn't as committed to me as he'd claimed. Years later, I considered myself lucky that it ended."

"Lucky why?"

"By seeing how the *love of my life* turned out. Michael is as big a jerk now as when we were teenagers. Why I didn't see it then is beyond me. Regardless of how angry I was at Logan, I have to admit that his butting in where he didn't belong saved me a lot of heartache later."

Too bad he didn't stay around to find that out. At first, she missed Logan so bad, Dakota thought she would never recover. It was during that time she realized that her attachment ran deeper than mere friendship.

"Hello?"

Dakota snapped out of her reverie. "Sorry. You know, it took me a while to get over it, but after retracing the events in my head, I convinced myself that Logan acted out of jealousy. I suspected that deep down, he loved me."

"And did you feel the same?"

She nodded. "Especially after that kiss. It felt like we had shared such a connection when it happened. That hope prompted me to go see him at college. He'd written me several times, but I didn't respond. Months passed before I realized I had to tell him how I felt, but that idea blew up in my face."

"Why?"

"Long story short, I went to see him and he was…he was with another woman. *With* her," Dakota stressed.

"Oh," Susan said sympathetically. She reached across the table and squeezed her friend's hand. "I'm so sorry, Dakota. I know what a rough time that was for you. I can't imagine having to face everything alone, and then to decide and declare your love just to have it—"

"Blow up in my face?"

"Not work out," Susan finished. "I know it must've been hard."

"You have no idea. Anyway, I returned home disillusioned, embarrassed and just plain numb. And that's the end of the story. I was stupid to think that Logan felt that way about me. I'd lashed out at him after learning the truth about Michael, and it was the worst argument we'd ever had. I told him to stay out of my personal life. We made up weeks later, and then out of the blue, he left. Each time he returned, it was tense between us. In retrospect, how can I fault him now for doing exactly what I'd asked?"

"Still, you should've told him about your visit and how you felt—among other things."

"What good would that've done? It wouldn't have changed anything I was struggling with at the time. No, it was better he didn't know I was there."

"But you'd have had the support you needed. A shoulder to cry on. You were heartbroken, Dakota. I'm convinced having Logan by your side would've helped you cope. Now there's a huge *what if* cloud hanging over the two of you."

"Oh, no, it's not." Dakota got up and began clearing the table. "There's nothing hanging between us, Suzy. Me and relationships don't work out. It's been a painful lesson, but one I've learned in spades."

"I disagree. I think you two should've cleared the air years ago. If for no other reason, it would ease the tension between you now."

"There's no tension."

Susan tilted her head to the side. "Were you not in the same room I was?"

Dakota placed the remainder of the Chinese food in the refrigerator while Susan wiped off the table.

"Look, there's nothing between us but a very lucrative contract, and I plan on upholding my end of it."

"If you say so." Susan walked over and hugged Dakota. "I'd better head home now." She grabbed her purse. "Have a safe trip, and call me the moment you land, and be sure to take plenty of pictures."

Dakota returned the hug. "I will."

She walked Susan to the door and watched as she got into her car and drove off.

Back in her bedroom, Dakota went over their conversation. She meant what she said. She had tried to mend her heart and find love again, but after a string of bad relationships, Dakota had decided that enough was enough. She would never give another person the power to devastate her again, and so far that plan was working.

Having to recount the details to Susan had been harder than she expected. It had left her a bit apprehensive about being in such close proximity with Logan again. Susan was right; they did have unfinished business that would need to be addressed at some point. How long could she put it off? They had never had a conversation about what went wrong between them. Each time Dakota got up her nerve, Logan was not around, or he had a girlfriend. The timing had never seemed right.

You need to relax. Being organized and having things "just so" usually did the trick, so she double-checked her luggage and travel documents. When that did not work, Dakota got into bed and turned on the nature-sounds app on her cell phone. The soothing sounds of babbling brooks, wind blowing through the trees and birds chirping always made her feel better. Taking deep breaths, Dakota closed her eyes and sank against her pillows. Tomorrow she would be meeting Logan in Jamaica, and her job would really begin. It would not bode well if she arrived at her assignment a bundle of nerves with bags under her eyes.

"Come on, girl, you've got this," she whispered. "Logan Montague is just another client, and you have a job to do."

By the next morning, Dakota was singing a different tune.

"Oh, no, I can't do this," she muttered to herself, but it was too late. She was already stuck, and being on a plane moments before it took off was too late to get cold feet. The little exercise she did last night to ensure that she could handle herself had gone south really quick. She was up for hours trying to convince herself that she could treat Logan like an ordinary client. By the time she drifted into an exhausted slumber, she was certain that everything would go off without a hitch.

The driver arrived to escort her to the airport, and now she was on board awaiting takeoff on a very impressive Gulfstream jet. She was very sleepy, but from the outside, she looked flawless. She was used to working with clients, traveling and long hours. Dakota always carried makeup and other provisions so that she looked pulled together.

She ran her fingers over the diamond Mickey Mouse pendant she was wearing beneath her blouse, rubbing it as though it were a good-luck charm. She scanned the inside of the plane. It was all about comfort. The plane's interior was a rich buff color with black accents throughout the cabin. Her club chair was plush leather with a table separating the chair across from her. There were two divans with small pillows flanking either side of the plane. A glass partition separated another area that had recliner chairs and television monitors. She saw a door beyond and wondered if it was a bedroom.

"Good morning, Miss Carson. My name is Angela, and I'll be attending you this morning. Would you care for something from the galley while we're waiting to take off?"

"Yes, some tea if you have it."

"Of course. Is there a specific kind you'd prefer?" Angela recited her choices.

"I'll take the breakfast blend, with cream, no sugar. Thank you."

"My pleasure, Miss Carson."

She wished she had a book or something she could read to occupy her time and calm her nerves. Maybe she could read an ebook from the Kindle app on her cell phone while they waited to take off. Dakota was scrolling through her selections when she heard Angela's voice again.

"Good morning, Mr. Montague."

"How are you, Angela?"

Dakota almost dropped her cell phone. What was *he* doing here?

"We're right on schedule, sir. Captain Tanner will be out shortly. Can I get you anything?"

"No, thanks."

Logan walked past Dakota's seat and sat down across from her. Dakota did her best not to look surprised when she gazed at him with what she hoped was a welcoming smile.

"Good morning, Dakota."

"How are you, Logan?"

"Well, thanks." He got settled, and then said, "Surprised to see me, aren't you?"

"A little. I thought you were at the resort."

Logan handed his briefcase to Angela and then fastened his seat belt. "I decided to wait so that we could travel together. Gives us a chance to talk before you get dropped into the thick of things."

She could not argue with his logic. She shifted in her leather seat. "Sounds good."

Dakota shut her cell phone off and placed it in her purse while Captain Tanner spoke to Logan about the flight plan and arrival time. He introduced himself on the way back to the cockpit, and assured Dakota that she was in good hands.

As she served Dakota her tea, Angela leaned in to whisper, "He says that every time."

"It's true every time," Captain Tanner called over his shoulder.

Angela blushed at being overheard. Dakota wondered if that was the real reason her cheeks turned pink. She could have sworn there was a lingering look between the two flight crew members. Dakota was surprised to look up and find Logan staring at her.

"I'm sorry," she said quickly. "Did you ask me something? I was lost in thought."

"No, you're fine."

When he made no move to elaborate, Dakota turned her attention to her cup of tea. She inhaled the strong aroma and cautiously sipped the hot liquid. Eventually, she began to feel more alert. She was almost done when the captain announced that takeoff was in a few minutes. Dakota busied herself with adjusting her seat belt while Angela carted away her cup and trash. Moments later, they were taxiing down the runway and were airborne.

She enjoyed the thrill of taking off. The sudden jolt of speed, the way she felt right before it left the earth. Landing was the same. When they had reached their cruising altitude, Angela came out to ask if either would like any refreshments.

"I'm good, thanks," Dakota said.

"I'll have a Pellegrino, Ange."

Dakota glanced over at him after Angela left. "So, what do your parents think about all the changes you'd like to make?"

Logan shrugged. "They're interested, but willing to let me run things as I see fit. I guess they're just happy I'm back in the fold."

"What have you been doing with yourself...besides taking over your family's business?"

He tilted his head to the side. "Are you really interested or just trying to make small talk?"

Dakota had actually been doing a little of both, but replied, "I wouldn't have asked if I wasn't interested."

Logan stretched his legs out in front of him. "I interned at Montague all through undergraduate school, and after I received my master's degree, I was offered a private-wealth position at a financial-security firm back in New York City, so I moved there. I made a name for myself in the business and financial industries, but eventually my familial duties came calling."

"So, it was a crash course in the day-to-day operations of running a resort."

"Not exactly. You forget I've been around it my entire life. There wasn't much I didn't already know about running Belle Resorts, but I wanted to incorporate its best practices with what I knew to be a successful business model. Despite the economic climate, our profits have remained steady, and we're holding our own. Still, I want to pull in a more diverse customer base and increase our sales."

"Have you thought about making one of the resorts all-inclusive, or couples-only?"

"No, but if you think that's the direction we should head..."

"I'm not saying that yet, but it could be a way to ensure that you're appealing to a broader demographic."

"Then I'm open to the possibility. As long as it's profitable and makes sense."

"What changed?" Dakota blurted out. "Years ago you couldn't wait to get away from the family business, and now you're back and CEO. What's different now?"

Logan's gaze captured hers. "I am. So, what about you? I would've thought you'd be married with some kids by now."

"Nope. I've been single for quite a while. I had a few relationships, but they didn't work out. And then…" She grew quiet.

He leaned forward. "What?"

She wanted to tell him, but now was not the time. "Let's just say that my life didn't exactly go according to plan."

When she did not elaborate, Logan grew quiet. A glumness wafted through the cabin, covering them both in a blanket of silence. It was deafening.

"How about you? I see you never got married or had children, either. Funny, I always pegged you as a family man. Was I wrong?"

"No, you're not wrong. I'd love to get married one day—and to have a family of my own, but I didn't want to settle for anything less than being madly in love with my wife and the mother of my children."

Dakota nodded. "Seems fair, so what's the problem?"

He shrugged. His gaze never left hers. "It seems I've been as successful as you have at finding my happily-ever-after."

"I don't know about you, but I've resigned myself that love just isn't in the cards for me."

Logan grew thoughtful, a small smile tugging at the corners of his lips. "Maybe it's time you changed the deck."

Chapter 5

"Oh, I've changed the deck a few times, but I never like the cards I'm dealt. Instead I decided to focus on work. That's the only gamble I'm willing to make," Dakota said.

"Like you, work became my focus, too. I know I was pretty vocal about my desire to go my own way, but time has a way of changing a man—and his outlook on life."

"I know what you mean."

"I found that the older I became, the more I realized that my parents needed me at their side. As their only child, I didn't have the luxury of being totally autonomous anymore. Despite the ramblings of a teenage boy, I realized that as a Montague, my loyalty was to my family."

"So that's when you decided to come back into the fold?"

"More or less."

"But I don't understand. Why come back to Chicago when your parents live in Florida?"

"I have family here, and history. Besides, it makes it all the more special when I go visit them," Logan replied. "Don't you agree?"

Her expression shifted. "Yes. I guess absence does make the heart grow fonder."

Logan knew something was bothering her, but before he could ask about it, Dakota began writing in her notebook. He recognized the avoidance technique from long ago and left her alone, but it was hard. She was hurting, but he did not know how to help her, or if she would even want his help.

Logan assigned himself a mission while on this trip with Dakota. His main focus was to get to know her again, and to fix the mess he had made of their relationship. If he plied her with twenty questions, he would get nowhere fast. Instead he would take a different approach by learning as much as he could about the woman she had become. What she liked, disliked. Her favorite food, and hobbies. From what he could see on the outside, she was enough to make any man's blood stir, and the more he saw her, the more he ached for some type of connection between them besides polite business associates.

He wanted back into her inner circle. Who knew how long it would take him to earn that privilege, but it would be worth it to see her smile at him like she used to. To see her face light up when he entered the room. To hear his name drift off her lips on a moan of pleasure—

"Logan?"

It took him a moment to realize that Dakota was speaking to him. He had gotten carried away with that last wishful thought.

"What? I'm sorry, did you say something?"

"You were looking a little odd. I asked if you were feeling okay."

He wanted to tell her the truth, but instead he said, "Yes, just fine. I guess it was my turn to daydream."

They continued on with general conversation until Captain Tanner announced that they were making their descent into the Ian Fleming International Airport.

"That didn't take long at all."

"Time flies…" Logan replied.

Dakota closed her eyes and concentrated on the landing. After they had come to a complete stop, she unfastened her seat belt and glanced out over the tarmac.

"Welcome to Jamaica."

She turned to Logan. "Hard to believe, but this is my first time here."

"Then we'll have to make the most of it."

He escorted her to an awaiting car.

"Is it usually this warm in September?" Dakota asked.

Logan nodded. "It's the hottest and most humid time to visit Ocho Rios."

"Great," she replied. "My suit is beginning to feel like it weighs a ton." She peeled off her jacket and undid two buttons on her blouse.

That wasn't nearly enough for Logan, but he refrained from comment.

The air-conditioned car was welcoming, and he watched her sink against the leather seat with a sigh of relief.

He eyed the dark pantsuit she was wearing. "I hope you brought lighter clothes."

She shook her head. "I can't believe I was so wrapped up in other preparations that I forgot to check the weather."

He noted that little confession did not sit well with her. "What's wrong?"

"I don't like anything slipping through the cracks," she told him. "It's not like me to forget to check on something this major."

"It's easy to believe that you were distracted. Especially since this arrangement came out of the blue for you."

She glanced up at him. "I don't get distracted."

With her mouth set in a thin line, he watched her observe the scenery out her window. Normally, Dakota had a devil-may-care attitude about things and would have laughed her forgetfulness off, but it was obvious to Logan that that was definitely not the case.

"Everyone gets preoccupied at some point, Dakota. Since when haven't you been able to see the humor in a situation?"

This time when she turned around, there was a stunned look on her face. "Was there humor in your up and leaving, Logan? I guess you'll have to tell me where it was because apparently, I missed it."

A pained expression surfaced on her face, but disappeared seconds later. This time it was Logan who turned away. He felt like an ass, and there was nothing he could say to the contrary. Fifteen minutes later, their driver turned off the main road, and drove down a winding path. It was flanked on either side with large trees, landscaped grounds and stone walls. Every few feet there was a copper lantern built into the masonry.

When the driver pulled up in front of the resort, he got out to retrieve their bags. Opening his door, Logan stepped out of the car and then held his hand out to Dakota. She placed her hand in his and allowed him to assist her.

"Thank you."

"You're welcome."

The tense moment dissipated, and Dakota's face transformed from annoyance to an appreciative smile.

"Welcome to Belle Cove," Logan said proudly.

"Thank you." Dakota surveyed her surroundings before eyeing the main resort. Painted a dark gray-green, it was surrounded on three sides by abundant trees and flowers. There was a large wraparound porch with wooden swings suspended from the ceiling. She turned to Logan. "It's…so beautiful here. I've seen plenty of pictures, but they didn't do this secluded gem justice."

"I'm glad you like it, but there's a lot more to see."

Logan escorted her into the reception area, and she was introduced to the general manager, Miranda Elliott.

Dakota shook her hand. "It's wonderful to meet you."

"Likewise," Miranda replied. "Is only good things me hear about you, Miss Carson. Nobody not saying nothing bad against you."

Dakota glanced at Logan, and then back again. It took her a few moments to follow the Jamaican lingo. "Please, call me Dakota."

"I really looking forward to the plans what you have for Belle Cove, but I kinda scared at the same time," Miranda confessed. "Is ten years I've lived here, and all the staff and guests is like family to me."

Miranda's voice shook with emotion. Dakota placed a hand on her shoulder in a comforting gesture.

"I assure you that my goal is to ensure that Belle Cove Resort prospers, while maintaining her core appeal."

Logan stepped forward. "Dakota can go into more in-depth discussions about her vision later, Miranda. Right now I'm sure she'd like to get unpacked and settled in. To-morrow is soon enough to start work."

Miranda smiled and swung her arm toward the door. "No problem, Miss Dakota. I'm more than happy to take you to the villa meself. Don't you worry yourself, every-thing irie."

Dakota moved to follow Miranda, but Logan's hand on her arm stopped her.

"Would you join me for dinner later?"

"Yes, of course."

"Great. I'll pick you up at five." He glanced at Miranda. "Take good care of her."

Miranda cocked her head to the side. "E'vryting criss."

Logan knew that meant all was well, so he winked, and then left.

As they walked, Miranda talked about the resort, where things were located and how many people were on staff.

Coming up on a brick pathway, she noted that it continued past the main building and into the lush greenery. There were so many things to see that Dakota slowed down every so often to look around.

"How many villas are there?"

"The main resort has guest rooms, a restaurant, activity center, the library, the staff quarters and lounge. There are six villas available for private rental—three one-bedroom villas, two with two and three bedrooms, and the last one boasts five bedrooms. All are accessed by a separate pathway, with private pools, gardens and plenty of privacy. The property backs to the beach, with cabanas, a pool, watersport equipment, a large pier, outside dining and a lighted trail."

"Sounds fabulous."

"Me can give you a tour, unless you want to go all about on you own? It's up to you what you want to do. You just let me know what is your pleasure."

"I'd love to walk around and explore, if that's okay?"

"Of course."

They stopped in front of a quaint one-story villa painted brilliant white. The large wooden door was wide open, and flanked by large blue ceramic pots with Jamaican wildflowers. Miranda stepped inside, and Dakota followed.

"Here we are."

Though it was extremely hot, all the doors and windows were open, and Dakota marveled that the villa was comfortable, and she could feel a breeze. Miranda told her that the entire house was less than one thousand square feet. The living room opened into the dining room, and off that was a small kitchen. There was a large printed sofa with two chairs with colorful accent pillows. Lots of local wood statues adorned the tables and walls, along with colorful artwork. Dakota walked into the kitchen. It had lovely dark wood cabinets and light countertops. Black appliances finished out the compact space. It was a bit dated, but otherwise it was a lovely space.

Miranda walked up behind her. "The path is right out back, and if you stay on it, it will take you to the dining area outside. If you go down further on the path, you will see a pool on the left-hand side. If you take the path to the left, you going to buck up on the beach."

"I can't wait to see them."

She followed Miranda to the master bedroom. A king-size bed dominated the room. There was an armoire along the right wall, and an open door that led out to a private terrace on the left. Her luggage had already been delivered, and was on a small bench at the foot of the bed. Dakota glanced in the bathroom, and then turned to Miranda.

"It's beautiful."

Her hostess relaxed. "Me be glad. If you be needing any'ting, you call. Enjoy."

"I'm sure I will."

Dakota went into the bedroom to unpack. When she was done, she took a shower and changed into a pair of leggings and a T-shirt. The lure to lay across the bed to rest briefly was too great to ignore.

A few minutes turned into an hour in record time. Dakota slowly opened one eye to check the clock on her nightstand. She felt as though she could sleep another few hours. The anticipation of the trip and all the excitement had clearly caught up with her. It took considerable effort, but Dakota made herself get up.

After washing her face, she went to the kitchen and checked the refrigerator for some water. To her surprise, it was fully stocked with juices, bottled water and snacks.

She also noticed a bowl of fresh fruit on the counter. She gazed around the room. *Was that there earlier?*

She still had time so she walked around her garden. Before she knew it, she had meandered down to the water's edge. There were a few people out and about, but not many. Dakota studied everything she laid eyes on. Eventually, it was time to head back. Reluctantly, she followed the path back to her villa. It did not take long for her to get dressed. She was in the living room putting on her heels when she heard a voice behind her.

"Are you going to wear that?"

Dakota's hand flew to her heart. She spun around to see Logan standing in her front doorway.

"Yes. Knock much?"

He walked in and sat down on the couch. "Most people just leave them open to take advantage of the tropical breezes. Usually, the only vacationers who close their doors around here are honeymooners."

"I'll be adding myself to that list." She paused. "Of door lockers, that is."

"You're going to bake in that outfit."

She glanced down at her navy blue skirt, matching jacket, white blouse and heels, and then to Logan's white linen pants and white short-sleeve top that was open at the neck. He looked as cool as an ice cube.

"Well, the only other clothes I have besides suits are lounge wear, and I'm not wearing those."

He stood up and motioned for the door. "Suit yourself," he joked.

"Give me a minute."

Dakota went back into her bedroom to grab her hobo bag. She took off her jacket and laid it across the bed before dropping her notebook into her bag. She closed the door to the terrace, but thoughts of returning to a stifling, hot house made her open it again.

She followed Logan outside.

"I see you left the door open," he said smugly.

"I didn't want to return to an oven. Where's the key to the place? I don't remember Miranda giving me one."

"You passed it on the way out."

Dakota looked confused, so he pointed. "It's hanging on a hook by the front door."

"So I take it security isn't an issue here?"

"No. We have a security staff that patrols the grounds, and I'm happy to say that there's never been an incident of theft here.

"Good thing I brought this," he said, sliding into a golf cart. "This might kick up a breeze and help cool you off."

Dakota rolled her eyes. "It's not that bad."

"Yet."

He drove them down the path that led to the beach. Logan stopped at one of the thatched-roof cabanas. Before he got out, he faced her.

"Dakota, I'm sorry for what happened earlier. I didn't mean to upset you—any more than I already have."

Dakota sighed. "It's fine. I shouldn't have taken my frustration out on you."

He walked around to help her out of the cart, but she had already slipped out of the vehicle. They walked down the path side by side.

"I thought we were going to be dining at the restaurant?"

"Dinner is coming to us tonight. It can get a bit loud in there. Especially with a full complement of guests in residence. I figured it would be better to dine out here. It's quiet, and we can talk."

Following him into the open-air room, she sat down.

"Wow, the table settings look very expensive and formal."

"Mom wanted guests to feel pampered when they dined."

Next, uniformed staff came in to set covered dishes down in front of them. She watched them complete their task and disappear into the back of the resort. Only one remained, hovering behind their table.

"Is it always this formal?"

"It has been for as long as I can remember."

"Hmm."

Logan regarded her. "Is that a good hmm, or a bad one?"

"It's just that…people are on vacation. They want to relax and be pampered, true, but that doesn't necessarily mean they want uniformed staff hovering over their table and enough china to warrant a photo shoot in *House and Garden* magazine."

"So you're saying that the waiter is making you uncomfortable?"

"No, it's not that. I think if you're dining with someone, you probably want to be focused on them, and not the person behind you."

"I guess it depends on the person, and the circumstances. Right now all I can focus on is you."

Chapter 6

A rush of heat suffused Dakota's face. Why was she blushing like a schoolgirl? *It is obvious that was his guilty conscience talking.* Her heart had something else to say on the subject. The compliment felt good, and she allowed herself to enjoy it for a few moments.

"I'm curious, Logan. How many times have you thought about me since you've been gone?"

"Every single day."

Well, that backfired. Dakota sipped the fruity concoction in front of her. It did a lot to dampen the sour taste in her mouth at his confession. Her heart was beating a conga line in her chest at his declaration, but she refused to make it that easy for him.

"You'd never have known that from where I was standing."

He went to open his mouth, but Dakota held up her hand.

"Logan, we should focus on work. I have a lot to do this weekend, and I don't need to be distracted by the past."

He nodded. "Fair enough." He held up his glass. "To the new and improved Belle Cove. By the time it's all said and done, I know you'll have exceeded my expectations."

Dakota held up her glass. "I'm up for the challenge."

They clinked their glasses.

She glanced past him and saw a small cat perched on one of the wood beams of the cabana.

"Look at you. You're so adorable."

Logan smiled at the compliment as Dakota got up and walked over to the railing. He turned and watched her talking softly to the feline.

He shook his head and got up. "That's Vagabond. He was a stray kitten when Tandie found him roaming around half-starved and in need of some nurturing. We took him in, got him food, made sure he was disease-free and vaccinated, and now he's the resort cat, though he still tends to roam around at night."

"Hi, Vagabond," she said before picking him up. "You're such a pretty girl."

"Guy," Logan corrected.

"A handsome man, huh?" she soothed, stroking his fur.

Logan walked over to the rail and scooped the cat up in his arms. "You get all the ladies, don't you fur ball?

"That's because *he* knows how to treat a lady."

He held his hand up to his chest, with a wounded expression on his face. "Ouch. What happened to just focusing on work?"

"Touché," she said, capitulating, "but you had that one coming."

They sat down and resumed eating.

"So," he said, changing the subject. "What do you think about dinner?"

"It's fantastic. I love the coco bread, and the jerk pork tenderloins are out of this world."

He held out his fork. "If you think that's great, try the red snapper."

Before she thought better of it, Dakota leaned in and took the bite of food. She smiled appreciatively. "That's delicious."

Logan watched her intently. He was mesmerized by the way her eyes closed, and a blissful sigh escaped her lips. He set the fork back down on his plate and ran his thumb over the knuckles of her hand.

Dakota stopped eating. Her gaze flew to his face.

"I want you to have a good time while you're here, Koty. I don't want everything to be about work. We have so much to offer."

Her eyebrows rose. "We?"

He didn't want to back down, but he promised he wouldn't push. "Belle Cove," he said slowly. "There's a great deal to see—and do."

The fact that she visibly relaxed wasn't lost on him. Logan would have to take things slower than he'd thought. Whatever it took to make her comfortable.

He sat back and took another bite. "Be sure and save room for dessert. We've got a bread pudding with a whiskey sauce that's out of this world."

"There's no way I'll have room," she groaned. "The food, breathtaking view and pampering are all conspiring to make me incredibly relaxed…and sleepy."

"It's too early to go to bed." He laughed. "And you haven't lived until you've strolled the property at night."

Dakota took a sip of her drink and nodded. "Okay, Montague, lead the way."

When they finished dinner, Logan gave Dakota the grand tour. Though it was early evening, the pathways were deserted.

They ended up sitting on a swing off the path in a secluded alcove. They rocked in companionable silence, until Logan leaned over and whispered, "Did I lie?"

She turned to face him. "No. This is paradise. I can

see how someone could fall in love with it the moment they get here."

"That's the plan. We want our guests to be return customers."

Dakota tried her best, but she couldn't hold back a yawn.

"That's my cue." Logan stood up, and then held his hand out to help her off the swing. "Let's get you home."

Logan escorted Dakota back to her villa.

"Good night, Koty. It's been a wonderful day."

"I agree, and thank you for dinner, and the tour. I had a great time."

"My pleasure."

Logan strolled back to his golf cart. Dakota watched him pull off before she went inside. She kicked off her shoes and plopped on the couch, barely stifling a yawn. The lack of sleep was catching up quickly. She wanted to call Susan to talk about the trip, but she was wiped out and opted for a quick text instead. Details could wait. Right now she wanted to slide into her king bed and sleep.

After her nightly routine, Dakota locked all the doors. A breeze floated through the windows, helping to keep it cool. Once she got comfy under the sheets, she pondered what tomorrow would bring. Would the staff mind her being there? Her thoughts drifted to Logan. He had been a gracious host, and so far was a great employer. It was obvious that he was going overboard to make her comfortable, but didn't most people when they wanted something? He may be saying all the right things, but Dakota's instincts still cautioned her to be wary when it came to letting him back into her life. Logan Montague had an agenda that went beyond what he was telling her, and she was determined to find out what.

The next morning, she awoke refreshed and ready to get to work. She was at the main resort by eight o'clock.

When she walked in, there was an older man at the front desk. Based on her notes, she knew his name was Tandie, and he was the night manager. He had a lively gleam in his eyes. She noted he spoke proper English with the resort guests, but when another Jamaican walked by, he switched to Patois, the native Jamaican Creole language. When he saw her, a smile lit up his face, and he placed a hand over his heart for effect.

"Mawning, Miss Carson. I'm Tandie Grey. Di heaven dem musta open up an drop a goddess from di sky."

Dakota blushed. "Thank you. That's the nicest compliment I've ever received, Mr. Grey."

Tandie had been at the resort since its inception, and was very close to the Montague family.

"You're just as beautiful as he described. He talks about you constantly, ya know."

Dakota did not need to ask who he was referring to. Instead, she switched topics and got Mr. Grey to talk about his job. She quickly found out that it was a subject that filled him with pride, and one he loved to share.

Later, she interviewed the landscapers, the chef and his crew, the waitstaff, housekeepers and the activity coordinator. She observed staff procedures, spoke with a few guests and got a tour of the other villas and guest rooms that were not in use. By the time she knew it, the day was practically over. Dakota was wiped out, but pleased at her progress. She was writing down some thoughts and speaking to Tandie when he jumped up and rushed to the desk behind them.

"Me so sorry, Mam...I mean, Miss Dakota," he corrected. "But me have a message fi yuh." Tandie handed her an envelope.

Dakota took the note. "Thank you."

He excused himself to attend to another guest. Dakota

opened the letter. Logan's bold handwriting was unmistakable. She read the message.

Meet me at the pier in ten minutes.
L.

Dakota glanced at her watch. She had five minutes. She returned the note to its envelope before sliding it into her notebook. Her feet hurt from walking around in heels all day, but she did not have time to go back to her villa to change shoes. With quick steps, she headed for the pier.

Logan was at the very end with his back to her. *Figures I'd have to walk the entire length of the wooden dock.* Her heels tapped out a loud cadence on the boards as she walked.

"Look at that," he murmured, not turning around.

She followed his gaze.

"Being here...at sunset...it's one of the most beautiful things I've ever seen. Right when the sun lowers on the horizon and sets." He pointed. "You see it? When I was little, Mom used to say that if I listened close enough, I could hear the hissing sound of boiling water right as the sun touched the water at sunset."

Dakota's expression grew warm. "I never knew that."

"I've never told anyone about it. Nor how old I was before I quit believing it."

After the sun dipped lower, he finally turned to face her.

"That must seem silly to you."

"Why would it? I think it's important for everyone to stop at some point during the day and just be still...to soak up the moment. Your time is sunset, that's all."

It was hard not to get caught up in the reverence of it. For a moment, she almost felt like she was intruding. She moved to take a step back and stopped. She tried again, and after a moment realized that she was stuck. Confused, Dakota glanced down and saw that her heel was stuck between two boards of the pier.

Trying not to draw attention to herself, she shifted her weight and tried to tug the leather pump free, but it wouldn't budge. *This is just great.* Dakota leaned forward, and as nonchalantly as she could, tried to raise her leg.

"So, how was your day?"

She stopped tugging. "Good. I uh…got a lot done today. Everyone was so helpful and pleasant. You've got a great staff, Logan."

"I know. They're the best. They're more like family than employees."

"I can see that."

"Have you eaten yet?"

"No."

Logan turned to walk down the pier. Dakota used the opportunity to bend down to try to wrench her shoe free. She was in the process of doing so when Logan turned around. He opened his mouth to say something, but then shut it. With a look of surprise, he closed the distance between them.

"Do you need help?"

"No, thanks," she said quickly. "I've got it."

Logan stood there and watched her try in vain to free herself. Finally, he kneeled down. "Let me help you."

"I really don't—"

"Dakota," Logan said softly.

She stopped tugging and gazed down at him. With a sigh, she held on to his shoulder for balance. He grasped her heel and tilted to and fro. Finally, it slipped free.

"Success," he exclaimed. Logan grasped her hand and helped her up before handing her back her shoe.

Dakota released him in order to take her other shoe off. She held them in her hand. "Thank you."

Logan grinned at her. "You're welcome. Did you want to get something to eat?"

"I think I'm going to pass. I'm kind of tired, and would love to just get a shower and go over my notes."

"Okay. If you're hungry, just call and my staff can have dinner delivered to you."

"I think I may take you up on that. Thanks."

"My pleasure."

Logan escorted her back to her place a few minutes later, and then said good-night. When she disappeared into the house, he strolled down the path to his villa. He sat down on the couch and put his feet up before running his hand over the stubble on his jaw. There had been a connection between them. He felt it the moment their fingers touched on the pier. If only he could get Dakota to acknowledge it. Most of the time she was serious and intense. It was a surprise to look down and find her toenails painted with tiny butterflies on them.

He smiled, thinking about how the whimsical design had shocked him. He wondered what else she was hiding that no one could see. *A tattoo? Body piercings?* Just imagining Dakota's bare skin made him shift uncomfortably in his seat. Needing a distraction, Logan picked up his laptop and checked his email messages. Aside from work-related mail, he had received a few from his family. He picked up his cell phone and dialed his cousin to check in.

"Hey, Adrian. What's up?"

"Hmm…let's see. You're out of town, so all my single friends are avoiding my house like the plague, just in case Mom stops by. There's no one else willing to take the bait and be fixed up, so you can imagine how much she's driv-

ing me crazy. To top it off, the deal I spent weeks working my butt off to close just fell through. Other than that,
just peachy."

"Sorry, man," Logan said sincerely. "Your mother definitely needs a new hobby."

"Tell me about it. She's on Dad's case to start a few
honey-do projects around the house. Needless to say, he's
not too happy right now, either. She got to babysit Ivan and
Tiffany's little boy, Gavin, so of course that only upped
the ante on her pitch for Milán and me to start a family. Look, enough about my nightmares, what's up with
work—and Dakota?"

"So far, so good. Today was her first day of evalua-
tions. I suspect she'll be pretty busy the rest of the time
she's here. Which doesn't give me much time to spend
with her…outside of work."

"Dude, you're in one of the most beautiful and romantic
places on the planet. You mean to tell me you can't find a
moment to put a log on the fire to thaw some of that ice?"

"Ha. At this point, I'd settle for a twig." Logan tried
not to let his pessimism show, but it was hard. "There's
no way she's going to relax her guard long enough for me
to make any headway."

"Logan, I don't mean to play Devil's advocate here,
but…are you sure you've thought this whole thing
through?"

"I'm not following."

"Well, you haven't really been involved with Dakota
since you two were practically kids. She's not the same…
you're not the same. You've both grown up. Are you sure
that your notions of her from the past will be able to meld
together with the realities of how she is now—how you
both are? I just don't want you setting yourself up for failure. You have to be prepared for the fact that no matter

how much you try, you two may not be able to get together. Maybe too much time has passed."

Logan steepled his fingers as he pondered his cousin's comments.

"I get what you're saying, and believe me, I'm scared as hell that diving into this may not work out the way I want it to. I'm trying not to have blinders on and to be realistic that my biggest hopes may not be realized, but...I have to try, Adrian. I can't live in fear of failure. I left before and convinced myself that the reason I stayed away was all due to bad timing, relationships and family obligations, but that's not all true." He paused for a moment. "Part of me was worried about what would happen if it *did* work out. I've wanted her for so long, and worshipped her from behind the safety of friendship, all while knowing just where that protective wall between friends and lovers was, and being careful not to cross it."

"But now you want to?"

Logan felt a mixed wash of apprehension and determination. "No, now I have to."

"I can't lie and say that I know one hundred percent what you're going through, but I can say that consciously deciding not to act is worse than taking no action at all. I'm here for you, man, and will help however I can."

"I know, Adrian. Thanks, cuz."

"My advice is to think about ways that you can mix a little pleasure with all that business. Find that happy medium that draws the two of you together. You'll find it."

Before he could reply, Adrian said, "Hey, I've got to run. Milán and I are meeting friends for dinner, and we're late. Remember what I said, Logan. You both have to get past all the boundaries. Peel back the layers and see what you have left. The only way Miss Workaholic will relax is if you make the fun time look like work."

Logan hung up with Adrian and pondered his advice. Adrian had a point. It was highly unlikely that Dakota would let her guard down long enough to enjoy herself, especially around him. She was wary of his motives, and he could not blame her. Still, he was determined to show her another side of himself. He was not the coldhearted, self-involved boy she remembered. He had matured and learned what was important and what was essential in his life.

There were plenty of things that were important, but fewer that were essential. Dakota definitely fell into the latter category, and Logan was determined to make amends. Though he was worried about how all of this was going to turn out, he was resigned to giving it his best shot. He was not going to lose her twice, and thanks to Adrian, he knew exactly what to do to get Dakota to lower her defenses—absolutely nothing.

"Have you met some tall, dark and incredibly handsome man yet? Preferably someone with a sexy-as-hell Jamaican accent?"

"No, I haven't. Not that I was looking, anyway. I'm pretty tied up with work. I don't have time to look for tall, dark and sexy-as-hell men."

"Are you crazy? Girl, every woman has time to look for a man that fits that description," Susan replied. "I take it all's well with Belle Cove—and working for Logan?"

"So far, yes. His staff is being cooperative, and I'm enjoying getting to know them and how they work."

"Still think you can handle everything?"

"Of course I do. Trust me, I know what I'm doing."

"I hope you're right. Now, just in case you do have an island fling, remember what I told you. Nobody ever looks better after more than three drinks, and practice safe sex no matter how good he tells you it feels without the condom."

Dakota blushed generously. "Susan."

"Don't *Susan* me. I know what I'm talking about."

She had to laugh at that. Susan was many things, but a well-seasoned party girl she wasn't. She did, however, have a very vivid imagination, and made the most of it.

"And on that note, I'm going to say good-night. My dinner is here, and I've still got a ton of things to do before bedtime."

"Work, work, work. Mark my words…you need excitement, Dakota Carson."

"I'll get plenty of it, I promise—as soon as I'm done."

"Uh-huh. Just remember, use it or lose it."

Dakota chuckled at that. "Good night, Susan."

"Night, Dakota."

A very shy woman named Amelie delivered her dinner. Dakota thanked her. After she left, Dakota moved her heavy tray to the dining room table. She removed the metal covers and stopped. She ran over to her notebook and wrote *metal covers* in it. When finished, she returned to peruse her meal of jerk chicken, red pea soup and a salad. She also had a delectable coconut-and spice-filled pastry for dessert called Gizzada.

Suddenly famished, Dakota dived into her meal with gusto. Afterward, she cleaned up, locked the door and went into the bedroom. She had just stretched out on the bed with her laptop when her house phone rang. Surprised, she leaned over and picked it up.

"Hello?"

"How was dinner?"

"Delectable, which you already knew. Amelie told me you picked it out. Thank you. Everything was amazing."

"Glad you liked it. Get much work done?"

"Yes, though I'm still at it."

"I was thinking. Perhaps tomorrow you'd like to drive into town with me?"

"I don't know, Logan. There's so much to do and not much time."

"True, but wouldn't it be helpful to check out some of the local artisans?"

He was right. Seeing what local design elements she could incorporate into her solution was essential to her renovations. "I guess so," she conceded.

"Great. I'll pick you up tomorrow at ten?"

"How about I meet you in the lobby?"

"Okay. I'll let you get back to work. Good night, Dakota."

She smiled. "Good night, Logan."

Dakota returned the phone to the nightstand. She felt silly. She had wrongly assumed that Logan was trying to ask her out on a date. She had wanted to shut him down immediately before he got any ideas in his head. Apparently, she was way off base. He had just been interested in showing her around town to help with her project.

It's just as well. She was his renovation expert, and nothing more. *What about the spark that shot up your hand when he touched you? Purely an isolated incident.* A residual connection to feelings long gone. Dakota did not have time to get caught up in teenage memories. Treating Logan like a colleague was for the best. If she let her guard down, it could prove to be disastrous.

"Fool me twice, shame on me."

Chapter 7

"Admit it, you had a good time today—even with me as your tour guide."

Despite her best intentions, Dakota laughed. "Fine, I agree. You're a good guide. There, are you happy?"

"I'm working on it."

Their very long and exciting day had started out with a coup. Both Miranda and Tandie had vetoed Dakota's outfit that morning.

Tandie shook his head. "Is dat wat yuh wearin? Yuh not gwen las fiv minits in dem heels yuh hav ahn."

"Or that suit," Miranda added for good measure.

They shooed her off to Belle Fleur. It was the lady's boutique at the resort. Dakota made a show of protesting, but secretly, she was not looking forward to another day roasting in her business clothes. Miranda must have tipped the saleswoman that she was coming because the minute she walked through the door, she was greeted with a friendly smile and a knowing look.

"Gud mawnin, Miss Carson. Mi name is Sophie and I gwen help yuh dis mawnin."

"Thank you, Sophie. I'm grateful for your help. I've lost about five pounds in water weight since Friday morning," Dakota joked.

"Nuh worri yuhself, miss. We gwen get it right like

rain. Evryting gwen criss." She escorted Dakota to the back of the shop and into a dressing room to try on a few selections. Dakota had a keen eye for fashion, and knew just by holding up an outfit what would look flattering on her frame. In the end, she chose a sleeveless, knee-length dress. It was white cotton, and felt cool on her skin. A pair of khaki shorts and a tank top, along with a sundress, completed her wardrobe. She gladly ditched her pumps for a pair of modest sandals. Sophie suggested a wide-brimmed hat since she and Logan would be doing a lot of walking.

Dakota was just about to pay for everything when she spotted a silver bracelet with two green turtles dangling from it. She picked it up. "This is beautiful. I'll get this, too." She slipped it onto her wrist while Sophie rang up her purchases.

"Yuh look beautiful…jus wait til Mr. Montague see yuh! Him eye gwen pop outta him head."

"Oh, I didn't buy this for him," Dakota explained. "He and I are just business associates."

Sophie did not bother to reply. Instead, she gave Dakota a huge grin and told her to have a great day.

One thing Dakota loved about the resort was that she could take one of the tree-lined paths and get wherever she needed to go. She walked from the boutique back to her cottage to put away her purchases and change her clothes. She picked the white dress and surveyed herself in the mirror before she walked back up to meet Logan.

He was waiting for her out front with Miranda and Tandie.

"Aren't you supposed to be off duty?" she teased him.

"Much improved," was all Tandie said before he nodded his head and strolled away.

"I agree," Logan replied. "And I didn't even see what you had on before."

"More suits." Miranda smiled, and went back to work.

"They overruled me this morning," Dakota explained. "Sophie was nice enough to help me find more suitable alternatives."

"Sophie is a gem, and you look beautiful."

Logan escorted her to his Mercedes coupe. He kept up constant chatter while he drove. Their first stop was to Wassi Art.

"It's a pottery studio that has a full-time staff of artists. Everything is original, and very colorful," Logan explained.

As they walked through the building, Dakota made notes in her book. She spoke with a few of the artisans, and inspected some of the pieces. From there, Logan drove her to Fern Gully.

"What's that?"

"It's a very scenic road with towering ferns on each side. It's like driving through a tunnel. There are vendors on the roadside selling their wares. I should warn you, a few have life-size sculptures of men that are…extremely well-endowed."

"Oh, really?" Her laughter filled the car's interior. "Thanks for the warning, I'll try not to stare."

Logan parked the car and helped Dakota out.

As they headed for the stands, he said, "You know, some will even let you take pictures with them."

"Uh, that's quite all right. I think I'll focus on the other attractions."

Logan started to laugh, and Dakota joined in.

She glanced up at him. "You know, you're enjoying this way too much."

"Me?" He grinned mischievously. "I don't have a clue what you're talking about."

Strolling past the sculptures, they focused on other

wooden carvings that were not so much of a conversation
piece. When they were done, he took her to a local design
studio featuring high-end furniture, textiles and fabrics.
Dakota felt like she was in a candy store. She roamed
around taking notes, checking prices and dimensions.

"Hey," Logan said, coming up to her. "We've been here
almost two hours, and I'm starving."

Dakota was kneeling down eyeing a tile. She stood up
and stretched. "Seriously? Wow, lost track of time. This
place is amazing. I could stay in here all day."

"How about a nice dinner out? I know a great place."

"Sure. Now that you mention it, I am hungry."

Dakota was following Logan out when several tiles
caught her eye.

"Dakota," Logan said, walking toward her.

"What?"

He took her by the arm. "Let's go before they charge
you rent," he joked.

"I can't believe all the great things they have here," she
said excitedly. "Some of these will be perfect for what I
have in mind. I'm so glad you showed me this studio."

"Me, too."

He took Dakota to Miss T's Kitchen on Main Street. It
was on a quiet cul-de-sac in a garden setting. While they
waited to be seated, Dakota looked around.

The restaurant was decorated in vivid red, yellow, blue
and green. It was outside dining that was casual and eclec-
tic. They were seated at a table near a tree strewn with
orange lights. It was converted from barrels while other
tables were hand painted with bright, bold designs. The
waiter welcomed Logan back before telling them about
the daily specials.

"I'm going to try something I've never had before," Dakota announced. "I'll have Miss T's Curried Goat."

Logan ordered the jerk chicken with ackee pockets.

"You'll have to try them. I bet you'll love it. Ackee is the national fruit of Jamaica."

"What's not to love? If the food is anything like the ambience of this place, I'm sure to enjoy it."

From the moment their food arrived and Dakota took her first bite, she was hooked. She closed her eyes and moaned in delight. "This is incredible."

"Isn't it? I try to stop in whenever I'm here."

Dakota ate everything put in front of her, and even ordered dessert to take back to enjoy later.

"I'll have to waddle back to the car," she exclaimed as she stood up.

"Not to worry. I'll go get the car and bring it to you. I'm sure waddling wouldn't be your best look."

She scrunched her nose at him. "I'd make it look glamorous."

"Uh-uh. That's not anyone's best look."

She waited patiently outside the restaurant while Logan retrieved the car. Once inside, Dakota stretched out in the seat and sighed. "This day has been amazing." She turned to Logan. "Thank you for taking me."

He glanced over at her. "You're welcome."

She rubbed her stomach. "How can you take it? I'm stuffed."

"I'm an old pro at it now. When I first tried Miss T's home-style cooking, I lost my mind. I ordered three entrées and ate every bite. That night I definitely waddled back to the car. I couldn't move for hours, but it was worth it."

Logan parked back at the main house, and then walked Dakota to her villa.

"It's the perfect night for a walk," she said on a sigh.

"There are many of those. That's one of the reasons I love this place. The beauty is beyond description. It's almost unreal how incredible this place is. The people, the scenery, the food—everything."

Dakota smiled into the darkness. "How poetic. You're quite the romantic. I bet your girlfriend considers herself very lucky."

"I'm sure she would…if I had one."

She turned. "You're not with anyone? Does your aunt know that? She's probably itching to fix you up."

"Constantly." He chuckled. "She is always on the look-out for my dream date. The Love Broker is relentless."

"Don't I know it," Dakota chimed in. "No is unquestionably not in her vocabulary."

Logan snorted. "Oh, it's there…Aunt Jeannie, please stop trying to fix me up. 'No,'" he mimicked. "Aunt Jeannie, I'm perfectly capable of finding my own dates. 'No, you're not. If you were, you'd be on one.'"

She burst out laughing. "You sound just like her."

"I've had plenty of practice," he said drily.

"And she's consistent."

"And she's consistent," Logan agreed. "I love her, though, and despite her crazy attempts to set up every single person within a three-mile radius of her house, she means well and just wants to see me happy."

"A long time ago, so did I," she confessed. "Now I just want to tie you down and throw eggs at you."

He stopped walking and faced her. "And I'd deserve every one."

Dakota gazed into his eyes. Seconds ticked by. "Well, not every one—especially not now. Besides, I could hardly terrorize my client with animal by-products, could I?"

"I guess not."

They walked in companionable silence. When they reached her cottage, Logan opened the door for her.

"Thank you…for everything today. I had an amazing time."

"My pleasure. Good night, Koty."

"You know, that nickname doesn't annoy me as much as it used to," she admitted.

Logan grinned. "Progress."

He went to leave, but she stopped him.

"So where do you stay when you're here?"

"The villa right behind you."

Her eyebrows rose. "Seriously? Why didn't you say something? You're my neighbor, and I didn't even know it."

"I wanted to give you your space. This way, you don't feel obligated to come over and see me."

She shook her head. Logan's teasing reminded her of better times between them. Part of her missed that a lot. "Ah. Good to know."

She spun on her heel and went inside. She walked straight through to her bedroom without bothering to turn on lights. Instead, she lit a few candles in her room, and took one into the bathroom. Dakota stripped down and took a long shower. When she was done, she put on a sheer nightgown and climbed into bed. She was about to blow out the candle by her bed when her phone chirped. She leaned over to see the screen. It read Sweet dreams.

Logan. She typed out You, too, and then turned it off. *You're supposed to be treating him with cool detachment, and not wishing him pleasant slumber.* The truth was, Dakota's wariness at Logan's intentions was starting to dissipate. They had found a way to work together, and that courtesy was spilling over into their nonworking relationship. She shook her head when she recalled Logan's words. "Progress."

Logan was too wired to sleep, and the pool at his place was not large enough to do laps, so he walked down the lit path to the beach. The roar of the waves hitting the shore was loud, but not overly so. The water was perfect. He walked into the water and immersed himself. Instead of swimming, he stood there gazing up at the moon and stars. It was a full moon that night, and it lit up the sky with pale light.

For the first time since he walked back into Dakota's life, Logan felt as if some of the ice had begun to melt. Now she smiled when she saw him and asked how he was doing. He may be taking baby steps, but at least it was forward momentum. Despite how much she would protest otherwise, Logan saw glimpses of the girl he used to know. She was not a total stranger to him. She still had some of the same mannerisms, likes and dislikes. He did not profess to know the innermost workings of her heart, but it was a start. At times, the glances she would give him were warm, friendly and companionable. Tonight, something else was there. Something unexpected. She had actually enjoyed being with him. He could see it in her eyes, and that made his heart beat faster. *Progress*.

Logan received a text message from Dakota the next morning saying she was at the cabana having breakfast if he wanted to join her. He got dressed and left.

"Good morning."

"Morning. That was fast. I just got here and gave my order to the waiter."

Out of nowhere, the man in question came up to their table. Logan placed his order and then turned his attention back to Dakota.

"Did he do that because you're the boss, or is he always so efficient?"

"Regardless of who you are, our staff's main focus is customer satisfaction."

She thought about Miranda and Tandie. "True. Everyone I've interviewed excels at what they do and makes you feel important."

"You are important."

When she lowered her eyes, he added, "As is everyone else at Belle Cove. It's one of the tenets my parents insisted on when they started the business. When you're here, you're family."

Dakota smiled. "I like that."

Logan watched her writing in her notebook. "What's in that thing, anyway?"

"My entire universe—at least as it relates to each project I work on."

When she stopped talking, Logan motioned for her to continue.

"It's every detail about what I'm working on. Employees, processes for the company, interactions with consumers, my thoughts…it's my work bible."

"Do you have one for every project?"

"Of course. Each client is different and deserves my full attention so…separate books."

Their breakfast arrived. Dakota surveyed her selection appreciatively.

"No pancakes?"

"Nope. I only want authentic Jamaican dishes while I'm here."

"Then you've chosen well. The most cherished meal here is breakfast. They celebrate their rich heritage with food that is filling, flavorful and delicious. Saltfish, ackee and callaloo are staples here. As is breadfruit, plantains and johnnycakes."

"Callaloo?"

"It's like spinach, but more robust."

Digging into her meal, Dakota sampled each item on

her plate. The fish was prepared with bell peppers, onions and tomatoes.

"Whoa, this has got some heat."

"It's the Scotch bonnet chilies. They're very hot."

"You're way better than the average tour guide," she teased.

"I've been coming here since Belle Cove's inception."

"True. I guess you're bound to pick up a thing or two."

"A mi fi tell yu!" he replied.

Dakota laughed. "Point taken."

"So, what's the plan for today?"

"Finishing up my site visit."

"You're just about done?" Logan was hoping for more time. "What's next?"

"Then it's back to my office to create the design brief. When it's ready, I'll schedule a meeting with you, and I'll present my concepts for revamping Belle Cove. We'll go over everything, along with any concerns you have at that time. After your approval, I'll head back here and begin setting up my team. Miranda provided me with a list of local contractors that have worked on Belle Cove in the past, so that will save us a great deal of time. I'm very excited about the project, Logan. I think you'll love my ideas."

"I don't doubt it."

She stood up and placed her notebook back in her bag. "I'm off to work. Thanks for meeting me for breakfast."

Before he could think better of it, Logan took her hand in his and kissed it. "Thanks for inviting me."

Dakota froze in her spot for a moment before she relaxed. "Sure. I'll uh…see you later."

She was gone before Logan could reply.

Great going, Montague. He watched her steady retreat. *Way to scare her off.* It had not been his intention to make her uncomfortable. He would have to catch up to her later and apologize. In the meantime, he had some work to do himself. He had a telephone conference in an hour. That gave him time to go for a run, and then shower and change.

With his decision made, he stepped out of the cabana and headed off down the beach. He thought of a few good uses for his excess energy, and Lord help him, every last one involved Dakota.

Chapter 8

My last few moments in paradise. Dakota stared out the window of the Montague jet. Soon they would be taking off, flying back to Chicago. Part of her was looking forward to settling in to her old routine. The other part, not so much. She would miss the breathtaking town on the coast, and Belle Cove. There was a relaxing, almost therapeutic nature to the resort. She had also experienced other emotions that had nothing to do with scenery, and everything to do with Logan.

He was not what she expected. He was calm, pleasant and helpful to her. If she was expecting a cocky, privileged and self-involved millionaire playboy, she was mistaken. Logan was none of those things. Sure, he was still a bit arrogant and sure of himself, but he was also kind, cared about his employees and went out of his way to be personable.

She had gone over it in her head last night and had arrived at a startling conclusion. She was actually starting to like Logan Montague.

"Holy cow," she breathed.

"Hey."

Dakota shrieked, and almost jumped out of her skin.

"Whoa, are you okay?" Logan asked, sitting across from her.

"Yes, sorry. I was just thinking about…work, and you startled me."

"Oh. My apologies." He fastened his seat belt. "To be honest, I was surprised to find you already here."

"Tandie was headed home and offered to drop me."

That wasn't exactly true. She had asked for a ride, but Logan did not need to know that. When she woke up, her emotions were a jumble. The last thing she needed was the source of that confusion inches away from her in a car overloading her senses. The plane ride home would be taxing enough.

"Dakota, what's wrong?"

"Hmm?"

"You're frowning."

"I'm not frowning."

"No? Well you're doing a very good impression. What's the matter?"

"I'm fine. I may be concentrating, but there's no frowning."

"Sure there isn't. So what are you concentrating on so hard that it looks like a frown?"

You. "Just work. I'm trying to plan out my schedule, that's all."

Logan's eyebrows rose. "In your head. I thought that's what your notebook was for?"

"It is, but I usually think over the preliminary stuff in my head first, and then transfer it to the book."

"You know, I don't remember you being this organized back in the day."

She shrugged. "A lot has changed since then. I'm not the same person. I've had to make changes—and sacrifices. That naive girl has changed forever."

"Forever? What was wrong with the person you were then?"

A shadow crossed her face. "That gullible teenager you remember is gone."

"You were many things, Dakota, but you were never gullible," he said quietly.

"Oh, please, what would you call it? Especially where you were concerned. There were how many maneuvers going on around me, Logan? I didn't notice one thing out of place."

"It wasn't like that. I...I only interfered in your life once. I swear."

"And that made it okay, right?"

"Of course it didn't. I was out of line, Dakota. What I did to you was wrong, and I take full responsibility for my actions. I never meant to shake your faith in me, and I should've stayed out of your relationship with Michael."

"Yeah, well, blind trust in others was one failing that I immediately rectified."

"So now you don't trust anyone at all?"

Angela walked into the cabin before Dakota could respond. Upset, she turned away and stared out her window. While their flight attendant was speaking to Logan, Dakota closed her eyes to keep from speaking to either one. She did not have faith that her voice would not shake, or sound like tears were barely held in check. The teenage version of herself had lived such a happy life, and now it was gone. In the blink of an eye, her world got turned upside down, and Dakota had been trying to right it ever since.

In one weekend, she had been swept up into forgetting the past. Into believing that she and Logan could have some semblance of a normal friendship. Dakota kept her eyes closed. She did not want to see him or hear his voice. The reminder of her loss was too great. Instead, she willed herself to relax and prayed that sleep would come to aid her escape. Moments later, it did.

How in the world had things gone from great to catastrophe in mere minutes?

One comment had caused a tidal wave to rise up and wipe out all his progress. He had somehow upset her, and could have kicked himself for the misstep. *Damn.*

She shut down faster than a roller coaster when it rained. How would he ever bridge the gap between them when one reference to their past wreaked this kind of havoc? It just did not make sense. Something was wrong, and Logan was now more convinced than ever that there was more to it than just his piece in the puzzle. Until they sat down and came to terms with the past, nothing he tried would work. He would never earn her trust, or win her heart.

Logan cast a glance at Dakota. It was obvious by her breathing that she was no longer faking, but really asleep. He needed to find another way to occupy his time. The last thing he wanted was for her to wake up and find him staring at her like a lost puppy. He got up quietly, and walked over to ease the pleated shade down to block the sunlight across her face. Afterward, he went in the back to watch a movie. Logan reclined in his chair, placed Bose headphones on and did his best to tune out the thoughts racing through his head.

Norma Jean had a family dinner every Sunday. Over the last year, the guest list had grown exponentially. In addition to her son and his wife, Adrian's best friend, Justin Lambert, and his wife, Sabrina, would attend, as would Milán's best friend, Tiffany Mangum, along with her husband, Ivan, and their son, Gavin. Since Logan had returned, he had made a few dinners, too. They had become her extended family, and permanent fixtures in the Anderson household. She loved every minute of it. Tonight she had decided to go Italian. She made homemade lasagna, a hearty salad, garlic bread and Dutch apple pie for dessert. Cooking was her favorite pastime, next to fixing people up. Norma Jean had been in the kitchen almost all afternoon. She was in her element.

"I'm going to need some help putting this extra leaf in the table," her husband, Heathcliffe, said from the doorway.

"Okay, honey. Give me a minute." She wiped her hands on her apron and went into the dining room.

"I hope this is the last thing on my honey-do list for a while—there's a *Lethal Weapon* marathon on television."

Norma Jean steadied her side, and her husband pulled his end. She helped him ease the table extender in place, and then they both pushed their sides back into place.

"Cliff, what does that have to do with anything?"

"I don't want to miss the first one."

"We have TiVo. Just record it."

"I am, but I want to watch it now."

She shook her head. "You are an exasperating man."

Heathcliffe walked over and pulled her into his arms. He kissed her soundly. "That's because you love me. If you didn't, I wouldn't get on your nerves half as much."

Norma Jean chuckled, but her smile was huge. "That's true. I was a goner the moment you asked to carry my lunch tray." She sighed aloud at the memory.

"That's not all I asked for," he reminded her. "I believe I asked for a kiss on the cheek."

"Yeah, but I wasn't giving you that. You'd better be lucky I had lunch with you. Imagine asking me for a kiss like I was some vixen."

"Well, you weren't then, but you are now." He winked and then left the room.

Norma Jean blushed and shook her head. "The things I have to put up with." She returned to her kitchen, but there was a bounce in her step.

Two hours later, Adrian and Milán showed up.

"Mom?"

"In the den, honey."

They took the containers they had brought with them into the kitchen and then returned to find his parents.

"What are you two doing?" Adrian asked when he spotted his parents on the couch watching television.

"Your father was all excited about the *Lethal Weapon* marathon."

"Dad, why didn't you just record it?"

"He did, but he wants to watch it now, anyway. Not like he hasn't seen it a hundred times since 1987."

"I love that movie," Milán said after she had kissed both of them. She sat down next to Norma Jean. "You know, Adrian has the whole set on DVD, if you don't want to bother with commercials."

"And ruin my snack runs?"

Adrian sat down next to his father. "That's true. I bet you have them timed out just right."

"You'd better believe it."

Norma Jean rolled her eyes.

"Mom, what can we help you with?"

"Nothing."

Both Milán and Adrian turned to Norma Jean.

"What?" they said in unison.

"Everything is ready. I'm just waiting on the rest of the crowd."

"Who's coming?"

"So far everyone. Your dad helped me put the leaf in, and we've already set the table."

The doorbell rang. Norma Jean got up.

"Mom, I can get it," Adrian replied.

"No, you sit right there. I've listened to your father's commentary long enough. It's your turn."

The Mangums were next to arrive.

"Hi, honey, you look lovelier each time I see you. It appears family life becomes you."

Tiffany hugged Norma Jean. "I'll say."

She took Gavin out of his father's arms and hugged him. "Oh, my goodness, what are you feeding this boy? Every time I see him, he gets bigger." She kissed Ivan on the cheek. "How are you, Ivan?"

"Just fine, Ms. Jeannie."

"And work? Gone out on any assignments lately?"

"I've cut down since this little guy was born. Tiffany doesn't like me having fun like I used to."

"If by fun you mean the time you went to Monte Carlo, and the man you were protecting almost got kidnapped, and you shot the kidnapper so he couldn't get away, then yes, I don't like when you do that."

Ivan hauled his wife to his side. "See, just like I said. No fun."

She eyed the plate of bite-size appetizers that Tiffany held. "This looks delicious, honey." She turned to Ivan. "I'm glad your wife puts her foot down. That's just what you need, Colonel Mangum. You own the company. It's time for some of your single operatives to go protect people. You've got a family at home to worry about."

Ivan looked properly chastised. "Yes, ma'am."

"Everyone's in the den. You all head back while Gavin and I get some plates.

"There's my little man," she cooed. "Now let's see what we can find in the kitchen, Gavin."

"That's the last thing I expected to see in your hands," Logan said from the doorway.

"Well, look who decided to remember where we live," she said in a singsong voice.

"Aunt Jeannie, I was here for dinner two weeks ago. Like I could ever forget where you live."

"Hmph." She walked over and kissed him on the cheek. "Which do you want? Baby, or plates and napkins?"

Logan stared at her for a moment, as if pondering the question. "Uh, definitely plates and napkins."

"What, are you worried you may get the urge to pro-create if you hold Gavin?"

"Definitely not." He laughed. "I just don't want *you* getting any ideas."

"Rascal."

Dinner was loud, fun, and Norma Jean loved every min-ute of it. By the look of happiness on her husband's face when their eyes connected across the dining table, so did he. After dessert, Tiffany, Ivan and baby Gavin were the first to leave, followed by Justin and Sabrina. Norma Jean made sure everyone had plastic containers with the left-overs. She was not wrecking her diet for anyone.

"Jeannie, don't you want to keep some for yourself?" Sabrina inquired.

"I'm not going to eat all this, and Cliff doesn't *need* to eat all this. Especially since he complains every time I in-sist he come to my senior water-aerobics class."

"I told you, that's because you're bossy. I'll let you be bossy at home, or at the community center...not both."

Norma Jean raised an eyebrow. "You'll *let* me?"

"Dad, quit while you have a chance. You are not sleep-ing on our couch," Adrian warned.

The only ones left thirty minutes later were Adrian and Logan. Milán was tired and had work in the morning, so Logan said he would give his cousin a ride so that she could leave. The boys offered to take care of the dishes.

"You and Dad go relax," Adrian told Norma Jean.

She immediately took her apron off. "Well, you don't think I'm going to say no to that, do you? Who knows when you two will offer to do dishes again?" She placed two pieces of pie on plates, kissed both of them and allowed Heathcliffe to drag her back in to finish *Lethal Weapon*.

After a few minutes of washing dishes together, Adrian looked over at his cousin. "So how are things going with Dakota? Have you made much progress?"

"Much? How about none. In fact, I've done the impossible—I've taken several steps backward."

"What? How's that even possible?"

Logan moaned aloud. "It's a sorrowful tale."

Adrian motioned to the dishes. "It appears we have plenty of time."

Not leaving anything out, Logan recounted his trip to Jamaica with Dakota.

"That doesn't sound too bad."

"Really? Because from where I'm standing, it's pretty bleak. She hasn't spoken to me since we got back…well, in person. She's sent plenty of emails."

"That's progress."

"All about work," Logan added.

"Hmm…I see your point."

"Face it, I've screwed up. There's not a chance in hell that we'll get back what we had at Belle Cove. She was warming up to me, Adrian. Now…it's back to the Arctic Circle."

"Logan, I'm married to a woman with a hot temper and a memory like a damned elephant. Believe me, I'm no stranger to deep freezes. I keep a parka in my bedroom closet for emergencies," Adrian said drily. "Trust me, we can fix this."

"I'm not so sure."

"The first order of business is to get your spine back. Stop being so negative. What happened to that man who blew into town hell-bent on winning Dakota back?"

Logan frowned. "I'm still here."

"Then act like it. With my help, you'll be back in her good graces in no time. If there's one thing I know, it's women."

Logan snorted. "This coming from someone who's slept on the couch?"

Adrian smiled. "I've never slept on a couch a day in my life. I said I have a parka in my closet for emergencies…I didn't say I've ever used it."

Norma Jean closed the door leading into the kitchen without a sound. She backed up and set two plates on the dining room table, then covered her mouth with her hand.

I knew it. Her instincts were telling her that Logan and Dakota had unfinished business. Alarm bells started pealing the moment she saw the look on Dakota's face when she mentioned Logan returning. She was not surprised, and there was another look in her eyes that Norma Jean knew all too well. Unrequited love.

Logan was back to win Dakota's heart. Well, she would not allow him and Adrian to screw it up. Dakota had been through so much in her young life and deserved happiness. They needed a pro at the helm. Half the work was already done for her oblivious nephew—Dakota loved him. Now it was time for the Love Broker to step in.

Chapter 9

"Are you going to tell me about it?"

Dakota looked up from her computer screen. "Tell you what?"

"Why all of a sudden you're in manic mode, and you haven't spoken Logan Montague's name aloud since you got back from Jamaica?"

"I've said his name."

Susan leaned on Dakota's desk. "No, you haven't—not once. And before you protest again, he hasn't been by here, either. So I can only assume that you're avoiding him."

Dakota opened her mouth to say something, and then closed it.

"Aha!" Susan cried. "I told you. Come on, spill it."

"It's stupid. I shouldn't have let it get comfortable between us again. I should've kept things strictly professional."

"But you didn't," Susan said eagerly. She sat down on the chair and scooted it closer to the desk. "You two had sex in Jamaica, didn't you?"

"What? I...no!" Dakota sputtered. "It wasn't like that. We just...had a conversation that I overreacted to. It brought back painful memories, that's all."

"Has it ever occurred to you that nothing has changed

because you won't let it? Dakota, it's been ten years. Cut the man some slack and level with him."

She reared back. "You're on *his* side now?"

"Of course not." Susan crossed her arms. "I'm your best friend. I'll always be in your corner. I'm merely saying that you're looking at this with blinders on, Dakota. You two were getting along in Jamaica. You can't convince me otherwise. It's time to move forward." Susan stood up and regarded her friend. "Give it a chance, Dakota. You can't see it, but you're stuck in place. You can't carve out the future until you've dealt with the demons of the past."

"So now you're a relationship expert?"

"No, but I have a more objective view."

She turned to leave, but Dakota's voice stopped her.

"I'll try, but…it's hard."

"I know," Susan replied before she left.

Great. She glanced down at her laptop. She was in distress, and Susan was right. She was just spinning her wheels and not going anywhere.

Dakota grabbed her purse and walked out of her office. "I'm going to be gone for a while, Suzy. If anyone calls—"

"I'll say you had an appointment."

Dakota hugged her. "Thanks."

"You're welcome."

Dakota could feel Susan watching her as she left. "Good luck," she heard her friend say softly.

The contents of the last moving box were finally put away. He was officially moved in. Logan glanced out the living room window over Lake Michigan. The view alone had sold him on his new condo. That and the north, south and east exposure. In each room, the entire wall was windows boasting unparalleled views of the city, lake and Lincoln Park. Logan sat down on the couch with his legs out in front of him. It was time for a housewarming. Maybe he would invite the guys over to watch a Bulls game.

Guys? What guys? Since he was out of touch with the people he knew before going off to college, his uncle Cliff, Adrian and his friends, Justin and Ivan, were it.

Maybe a party? He knew his aunt would be more than happy to help him pull something together.

Logan was about to call her when the phone rang. He leaned forward and picked it up from the coffee table.

"Hello? Really? Yes, I do. Sure. Thank you."

Logan hung up from speaking to the doorman, and bolted off the couch. He spun around 360 degrees to survey the area. Everything was in place. With a sigh of relief, he glanced in a nearby mirror, and decided to go change his shirt.

When his doorbell rang, Logan went to open it.

"Dakota."

"Hi, Logan. May I come in?"

"Yeah, sure." He stepped aside. "Welcome to my humble abode."

Dakota tried in vain to keep the surprise out of her voice. His *humble abode* was a lakeview condo in one of the most sought-after residential buildings in Chicago. "This is an incredible apartment, and killer view."

"Thanks."

"I hope you don't mind me coming by."

"No, of course not." Logan motioned to the couch. "Please, make yourself comfortable."

She followed him and sat down.

"Can I get you anything? I don't have much by way of food. I haven't done any real grocery shopping yet, but I do have soda, water, iced tea and beer."

"Water would be fine."

She looked around while she waited. From what she had seen so far, the furnishings were very high end. The hardwood floors were wide-planked Brazilian cherry. Since it was an open floor plan, it made the space seem enormous. With a wall of windows and neutral decor, it was bright and inviting.

"Here you go."

She accepted the Pellegrino. "I thought you only drank this on your plane?"

He grinned. "Nope."

They sat down on the sectional couch. Logan turned sideways to face her.

"I'm surprised to see you. Not that I didn't appreciate your keeping me in the loop with emails."

She shifted uncomfortably. "You're right, and it's completely my fault."

"No, it isn't. I guess I get under your skin sometimes."

"I think the problem is that you never left. I've been carrying around all this baggage for the longest time. I know it must be confusing, but it's not all you."

"Would it be better for you if I got someone else to do the renovations on Belle Cove? It's obvious I never should've put you in this position and I—"

"No," Dakota said quickly. "Unless you're unhappy with my work?"

"Of course not. I loved your design briefing, and there's nothing I'd change. I want you at the helm of the renovations, Dakota, I always have, but I don't want you to be stressed out having to work with me. I've caused you enough pain."

"You've been nothing but patient since our flight home. I've been totally unprofessional, and I apologize, Logan."

"There's no need. Though I would like us to be able to circumvent this…impasse."

"Me, too. That's why I came. To apologize, and to explain some things."

"Okay."

"First I need to know *why* you sabotaged my relationship with Michael."

He took a deep breath and sat back against the seat cushions. "I never thought he was worthy of you. Ultimately, I realized that wasn't my call to make, but back then, I was arrogant enough to think I knew what was best for you—who was best for you. I never should've interfered, and that night when we had the big argument about it—let's just say it was the second worst night in my life."

She glanced over at him. "What was the first?"

"The night I left town."

"Why did you leave, Logan? Really?"

He expelled a tortured breath. "My father laid on the emotional blackmail pretty thick. He wanted me to start learning the ropes so that eventually I could take over. I had big plans to step outside of the path my parents had chosen for me and to do my own thing, be my own person, but that went up in smoke. After the boyfriend debacle, it was easier to tell myself you'd be better off without me."

"Why would you think that? Sure, I was mad at you, but we'd gotten past that. Why did you even think it was still an issue? Especially after our last night together? Besides, have you seen Michael these days?"

"Uh, no."

"Well I have, and trust me, you did me a favor. It never would've worked out for Michael and me long-term. We were totally different people."

"That may be true, but I still shouldn't have hindered things. I told myself that it was for your own good. There was a connection between us, Koty. A strong one. I didn't want anyone to ruin that."

"So you decided to ruin it first? Do you have any idea what your desertion did to me, Logan? I was devastated."

He ran a hand over his face. "I never wanted to hurt you, but I suddenly found myself unable to be around you," he finally admitted. "Not without telling you how I truly felt. I liked you, Dakota. Much more than a best friend should, but I'd convinced myself you'd never feel the same. And when we kissed, I told myself you'd think it was just a goodbye kiss, but it was so much more—at least on my end."

Dakota went still. There was so much to process, and it was overwhelming. *He had feelings for me.* Years ago, that was all she had wanted to hear. Often Dakota would lie awake at night, wanting, praying and waiting for those words. Now he had said them, and she had no idea how to feel about it. She stared at him with such regret. "I can't believe that you…you were a bigger jerk back then than Michael ever was."

"I know."

"Not once did it occur to you to ask me how I felt? Why didn't you talk to *me*, Logan? You're supposed to be my best friend, you're supposed to be able to tell me anything, and you just assumed that I'd never reciprocate your feelings—even after you kissed me and asked me to wait for you?"

"I admit it, I messed up. I went about things all wrong."

"I *did* care about you, Logan, and I'd have done anything to hear those words in return. Then you left, and my life changed forever."

When she stopped, he leaned forward. "How? Talk to me, Koty. I know you're holding something back—I can feel it."

She stood up abruptly. "I'm sorry, I came here to tell

you everything, but now that I'm here, it's too much. I…I can't do this."

She grabbed her purse and raced to the door. He was off the couch in an instant. Logan blocked her path. He held his hands out to calm her.

"Koty, wait. Please don't leave—not like this. Whatever it is, let me help you."

"You can't."

"You're too upset to drive. Please, just wait for a bit. I'm not going to pressure you to talk about anything. We can sit here in absolute silence if that's what it takes. I just don't want you getting into a car when you're this emotional, okay? Whatever it is, we'll fix it, I promise."

"You can't fix it. Nobody can fix it," she cried. "I wish to God I could go back to that night and stop it."

"Stop what?"

She was shaking with pent-up grief. Finally, it bubbled over like a geyser. "My mom and dad…Logan…they're dead."

Shocked, Logan's hands dropped to his sides. He just stood there. "What? No."

She nodded. "We stopped at a convenience store. Mom wanted to bake something, but for the life of me, I don't remember what. She asked me to go in, but I was on the phone and didn't want to, so she went instead. Moments later, there was a commotion. Two guys were trying to rob the store. They had rounded up the customers and stood them against a back wall. It all happened so fast. Dad told me to stay in the car and call the police. While I was doing that, he…he told me he loved me, and to sit tight. Before I knew it, he'd run into the store. I screamed for him to come back, but he didn't stop. He wrestled one guy to the ground and tried to get to my mom, but the man shot him. That's when Mom screamed and ran over to help my dad, but it was too late. He was gone. She—she was in such a rage, she charged the one that shot Dad and he—that bastard killed her, too."

"Oh, my God. And you saw it happen?"

Tears streamed down Dakota's face as she recounted the grisly scene and the horrific aftermath.

"Yes. By then I heard police sirens. They ran out of the store. They didn't see me, but I saw them. They were apprehended a short distance away. Several of the witnesses and I testified at their trials."

"You testified?"

"Damned right I did. They were repeat offenders, and I swore I'd be there to make sure they answered for what they did to my family," she said forcefully. "My parents would not die in vain while their killers roamed the streets destroying other families. I was at trial every single day. When they were found guilty of murder in the second degree and sentenced to life in prison without parole, I went into the courthouse bathroom and cried."

The thought of Dakota facing down the violent men who killed her parents made Logan's blood run cold. He took her in his arms. "Koty, I'm so sorry. I…I didn't know."

"There were so many times I wished you were here," she cried. "There were some days when the pain was so great, I thought it would crush me. Even though the robbers were never getting out, I hated the fact that my parents were dead, while the monsters who took their lives were still here living…breathing…pumping iron in the yard. I know I'm supposed to forgive, but they didn't deserve to die like that. What's wrong can never be made right again, and I'll live the rest of my life knowing that my mother's death is on my hands."

"Whoa, wait a minute. Dakota, you can't blame yourself

for this. The guys who held up that convenience store were the ones who set this horrible tragedy in motion, not you."

She wrenched herself out of his arms. "I should've been in there, not out in the car on the phone. I was too stupid and selfish to do the one thing my mother asked of me, and she paid for it—with her life. My father, too. There's not a day that goes by that I don't wish they were here with me—instead of me."

Logan's jaw tightened. "Dakota."

"I wish I could take back what happened, to make amends for the part I played in their deaths, but I can't. And the pain never goes away. It's here with me every day. Sometimes, it's all I can do to get out of bed. Even now, years later, to open my eyes and face the day without them is bad enough without every birthday, anniversary and freaking holiday being a constant reminder of what I don't have anymore—and never will."

Logan wrapped her in his arms again and held her as though life depended on their connection. That's when her self-control slipped completely away and she cried and cried. He picked her up, and sat down on the couch with her still in his arms. He held her until there were no tears left, only empty shudders.

"I'm so sorry, Koty. I should've been here for you. I wasn't—when you needed me the most." Logan's voice shook. "I'll never be able to make that right."

"I hated you so much back then." She sniffed. "I hated you for leaving, for not coming back, for not knowing that my parents died. For not being there for the funeral, or any of the days in between."

"Why didn't Aunt Jeannie or anyone call me? I would've been here no matter what was going on," he said vehemently.

"I asked her not to."

He set her back so he could see her face. "Why?"

"Because I needed to be angry at you. I wasn't ready to let it go. Deep in my heart, I knew that if I made you the bad guy, that it would make me feel better about myself. About what I'd done."

"You didn't do anything. Listen to me. It was a random act of violence that no one could've predicted. You were just a teenager when it happened. Nobody blames you, and it's time you quit blaming yourself."

Silent, Dakota turned away from him.

He got up and went to the bathroom. When he returned, Logan was carrying a damp washcloth.

"Sit back and close your eyes."

She did as he asked, and he placed the cool cloth over her face.

"I must look a fright."

"You look beautiful."

She moved the cloth so that she could see him. "You're lying, but thank you—for being here."

Logan caressed her face, wiping the tears away with his thumb. He kissed the tip of her nose. "I'm sorry I'm late."

A small smile crept up her cheeks. "Well, you're here now. That's all that matters."

"And I'm not going anywhere, Dakota. I promise."

She laid back against the cushions. "I'm sorry, all of a sudden I feel wiped out."

Logan got up and scooped her up in his arms.

"What—?"

"Shh. I'm taking you to my bedroom. You need to get some rest."

"You don't have to do that. I—"

"Will be lying down," he finished for her. "No buts."

She yawned. "I feel like an elephant has sat on me, and my eyes are about to explode."

He picked up the remote and closed the blackout blinds on his windows. "Do you want some Tylenol?"

She yawned again. "No, just a nap."

Dakota kicked her shoes off and slipped under the covers. "Thank you," she whispered.

He squeezed her hand. "Anytime."

Before he got to the door, Dakota called out.

"What's wrong?"

"Nothing." She yawned. "I'm glad you're here, that's all."

His mouth tipped up into a smile. "Me, too. Now get some rest. If you want, we'll talk later."

She laid her head on the pillow as he closed the bedroom door. When he checked in on her minutes later, she was sound asleep.

Logan walked over to the window. The bright sunlight streaming in made his eyes hurt. Right now, his heartache felt as vast as Lake Michigan. A gut kick would have been less painful than watching Dakota recount her story, and the helplessness he felt listening to her world fall apart. A world that he should have been a part of.

When his cell phone rang, he ignored the call and let it go to voice mail. The phone rang again minutes later and again shortly after that. Each time he let it go. The fourth time, he stalked to the table and answered.

"Hi, Aunt Jeannie," he said in a voice devoid of emotion.

"Saints preserve us. I was going to ask you how things went with Dakota, but I already know."

"She…she told me everything."

"Oh, honey. Are you okay?"

"Not really. I feel like a jackass. She had to relive that nightmare all over again tell me what happened. Aunt Jeannie, when I left, I was only thinking about the path I needed to take for *my* life. I told myself that Dakota would be okay. She would go to college, make friends and have everything her heart desired in life. But the truth is, she was drowning in tragedy, and I was living the high life and nowhere to be found. And what makes it so hard to take is that not one of you told me what was going on."

"You're right, Logan, we didn't. Because Dakota asked us not to."

"This shouldn't have been kept from me. I wasn't there for her, and now her trust in me is broken. I can't fix that, Aunt Jeannie."

"I'm sorry about not telling you, but it's not too late, Logan. Everything can be fixed."

Logan would not allow himself false hope. "Not this. I've ruined any chance I could've had with Dakota. I came back here all confident that I would win her over. I'd get her to work on Belle Cove then declare my love and sweep her off her feet," he said with remorse. "I'm ashamed of myself."

"Honey, you've had a major setback, and things are not the nice, neat package you assumed they'd be when you returned. Yes, you've got some serious work to do, Logan, but I know you'll do whatever you can to fix your relationship and heal Dakota's heart. The thing about women is…you have to show us, not just tell us. We love words, Logan, but we also need deeds."

"I hear you."

"And the one thing I know about is love. It's stronger than fear, doubt or anger. Don't worry, you two will find a way."

"I appreciate your advice and support, but do you mind if I call you later?"

"Of course. Let me know if you need anything."

"I will."

After ending the call, Logan lay down on the couch.

He was emotionally exhausted, and needed to regroup. Dakota had given him a great deal to process. His world was tilted on its axis right now, and he wasn't sure what the best approach would be to restore the balance. She had feelings for him. He did not imagine it. She said that she had cared about him as more than a friend, too.

His heart had hammered inside his chest at her tortured words. Dakota's confession was both a blessing and a curse. It was all he had ever wanted to hear, but it also scared him to death. His deep-rooted fear that had they been together, he would have failed her somehow, was real. It gnawed at his confidence then, and made him second-guess if he was on the right path now.

When his eyelids grew heavy, he welcomed sleep. An escape from the pain of the afternoon's revelations and what they implied was exactly what he needed. He would regroup and figure out what to do later, but for now, he had no clue. The only certain thing was that he would be there in whatever capacity she needed him. He would never fail Dakota again.

Chapter 10

"Okay, what are you up to?"

"Me? Nothing, why?"

"Jeannie, I've been married to you long enough to smell a setup a mile away…and you're smiling to yourself. When that happens, someone's on your radar."

She shook her head. "Cliff, really. Why can't I just be in a good mood?"

"You know, I'm not sure. Why *can't* you just be in a good mood?"

"Because those two definitely need my help."

He sighed loudly. "Which two?"

"Logan and Dakota."

"Oh. Oh," he repeated, drawing the word out. "I'd stay out of it, Jeannie. There's a lot going on there."

"Don't I know it?"

The doorbell rang. Norma Jean turned to her husband. "Would you get that, sweetheart?"

The second Heathcliffe was gone, Norma Jean picked up the phone and dialed Dakota's office.

"Hi, Ms. Jeannie," Susan said. "I'm sorry, Dakota's gone for the day, but I did leave her the message that you called earlier."

"I know, but I was wondering if both of you are free to come to dinner at my house next Sunday. To be honest, I'm thinking of redoing the den for Cliff. You know, turn it into one of those newfangled man caves. I wanted her to look it over while she was here. It's a surprise, so I thought why not invite everyone over for dinner. That way he doesn't suspect anything."

"Dakota's schedule looks clear, but I'll have to check with her first. She does have Belle Cove, and another client at the moment...."

"I'm only looking for some suggestions, no major renovations. Just pick-your-brain type stuff on decorating tips. I'm sure that won't be too much for her."

"Okay. I'll let her know."

"You'll be able to make it, too, won't you?"

"I'm sure I will. Thanks for inviting me, Ms. Jeannie."

"You're welcome, dear. I'll see you Sunday."

Norma Jean hung up the phone and returned to her crocheting. Sometimes it was hard to lead a horse to water and get him to drink, but she had a way of coaxing the steed so that by the time she was done, he'd never go thirsty again.

If she could bring happiness to her son, the avowed bachelor, surely she could help Dakota and Logan bridge the gap of hurt feelings and unconsummated love. One thing was for sure: she would try.

Heathcliffe returned, and she asked him who it was.

"Some kid selling chocolate bars for their school's fundraiser. Like we need any chocolate bars."

"How many did you buy?"

"Six, but that's not the point."

She hid her smile behind her crocheting.

"Back to our conversation. Jeannie, I'd tell you to butt out, but I know that's a snowball's chance in hell."

"You worry too much, sweetheart."

"Uh-huh. That's the kind of stuff you say right before

the matchmaking storm rolls in. I think it's high time you retired and found a new hobby."

"I've got plenty, thank you."

Heathcliffe glanced up at the ceiling and then back to his wife. "You know, over the last forty years I've learned to pick my battles." He bent down and kissed his wife soundly on the lips. "Time for bed, beauty."

"I'm not sleepy, Cliff. Plus I'd like to get further along in my blanket."

"Who said anything about sleeping?"

His gaze captured hers for a moment, and then he sauntered out of the room.

"Oh, really?" she called behind him. One thing she could definitely say about her husband—Heathcliffe was never boring.

Norma Jean put her yarn and needles into the basket by her chair, and after hitting the lights, followed her husband upstairs.

Dakota stirred and slowly opened her eyes. They burned, causing her to blink a few times to see. She was in Logan's bed, and several hours had passed. The blinds were closed, but it was after five, so she knew it was already dark out.

Swinging her legs around, she got up and padded to the bathroom to rinse her face. Dakota dried it on a hand towel and went out to find Logan.

She spotted him stretched out on the sofa sound asleep. She sat on the side of the couch farthest away from Logan so she would not disturb him. Drawing her legs under her, she sat and stared at the flickering lights of the city.

Her head still hurt, but telling Logan about her parents was long overdue. Though drained emotionally, she felt better overall. There was still the visit to see him in college that she left out, but she was not ready to confess that yet.

"Hey."

Dakota glanced over to see Logan awake and sitting up. "Hi."

He got up and went to sit by her side.

"How'd you sleep?"

"Great. Looks like we both needed to recharge."

"True. Are you hungry?"

"Kind of."

He got up and went into the kitchen. He opened a drawer and took out a handful of menus. "I don't have much in the house, but we've got loads of choices for dinner. What's your pleasure? Indian, Thai, Greek, Southern or barbecue?"

"Okay, you're making me really hungry." She laughed. "How about a pizza?"

"You were trying to trip me up, weren't you?" Logan held up another menu triumphantly. "But I've got you covered."

He came back and handed it to her. "Lady's choice."

She scanned the menu. "The white pizza with chicken, and an order of the cheese breadsticks, please."

Logan looked surprised.

"What? You didn't think my obsession with white pizza would just go away, did you?"

"No, of course not. I'm actually happy to know that you still like it. Me, too."

He went to get his phone and place their order. When he returned, he was carrying a glass of wine and a beer. Logan offered the wine to her and sat back down.

"You didn't mention wine earlier in my list of beverage choices."

"I'd forgotten about it. It was in the wine room."

"What?" She glanced around. "You have a wine room?"

"Well, actually it's more like a wine pantry. It's not well stocked. I believe there are two bottles in there. Correction." He grinned. "One bottle."

They caught each other up on lighter times in their lives while waiting for the pizza to arrive. Dakota admitted that a few of her favorite things were the thirty-seven pairs of heels in her closet, watching WWE Divas on television and baking designer cupcakes. Logan confessed he was a diehard fan of racing, and it did not matter what. Cars, horses, ATV's, motorcycles, boats.

"Ah, a speed demon, huh?"

"I'll admit I have a certain affinity for going very, very fast."

"You don't bet on all of those, do you?"

"No. Maybe an occasional football or basketball game, but that's it."

"Okay, what other guilty pleasures are you hiding?"

"Donut holes, and playing Call of Duty."

She smirked. "The donuts I get, but since when have you liked video games?"

"I'm a man. Since when *don't* we like video games?"

His home phone rang. When he hung up, he said, "The pizza guy is on the way up."

Dakota got up and went into the kitchen. She looked around for plates and napkins while Logan paid the delivery man. When he returned, Dakota had set up everything at the dining room table.

"Thank goodness you had granulated garlic powder, or I would've had to send you out to get some."

"That's right, you're a garlicaholic." He set the pizza between them. "Do you still put it on everything?"

"Almost everything."

They compared best jobs, worst bosses and last ones

before going into business for themselves. Dakota told Logan about the Rothschild sheets conundrum.

"It shouldn't be too hard to find him. Do you want me to see what I can dig up?"

"And ruin Susan's fun? She thinks she's an operative on a covert assignment."

"Okay, but keep me posted."

When they were done eating, Dakota insisted on cleaning up, but Logan refused.

"Don't worry about it. I'll take care of it later."

She stood up. "I should be going. Thank you, Logan, for today. I'm glad I came here, and that we cleared the air."

"I'm glad, too." He hugged her tight. "Call me anytime, day or night, if you need to talk."

"I will."

"I mean it. I'm here for you, Koty."

Dakota nodded. "I never thought you would be again—but thanks."

He watched her walk down the hall and out of view before closing the door.

After tidying the kitchen and putting away the leftover food, Logan returned to the living room and flipped on the television. He put his feet up on the coffee table and tried to clear the rampant thoughts swirling around in his head. He was still reeling from Dakota's revelations, and being able to open up with her a little to share some of their personal stories. It spoke volumes about their progress.

He was still sitting there when Dakota texted him an hour later.

I'm home. Safe and sound.

Good, I'm glad. Sleep well.

I definitely plan on sleeping in tomorrow.

If I remember correctly, *in* for you is eight in the morning.

True, but that's a big deal for me.

They said good-night, and he set his phone down. Normally, he would turn it off, but he decided to keep it on. He knew it was a stretch, but if Dakota ever needed to call him, he wanted to be available. Now that she had given him the opportunity, he was not going to let her down. He was confident that things would even out, and they could rebuild their friendship.

"How long are you going to let your hair grow?"

"Huh?"

"I'm just wondering if it'll be as long as most bonafide hermits, or do you intend to keep it at a reasonable length?" she joked. "I've missed seeing my buddy—outside of work, that is."

Dakota set her notebook aside, got up and gave her best friend a hug. "Very funny. I'm sorry, Susan. It's been crazy lately, but in a good way. Belle Cove's renovation is coming along, and as soon as we can, girls' night out!"

"I'll drink to that," Susan replied.

"So what's the latest with the report on the Rothschild sheets?"

"Good news," Susan said excitedly. "I've got a spa day appointment downtown on the day Bootsie Ellerby will be there. My plan is to strike up a conversation, casually drop the sheets in there and then watch her tell me all I need to know."

"Susan, that's a great idea." Dakota hugged her. "Thank you. I won't ask how you found out Bootsie's schedule."

Susan grinned conspiratorially. "You'd be surprised what you can find on social media—speaking of social, Norma Jean's dinner party was fun, wasn't it?"

"Yeah, it was, but then they always are."

"It's nice sharing good food and even better conversation, don't you think?"

With a smirk, Dakota set down her pen. "Okay, where are you going with this?"

"So have you—"

"No, I haven't," Dakota finished for her.

"I'm just saying, I'm sure it would be better if you two were at least cordial."

"Logan and I are plenty cordial. We talked at Ms. Jeannie's, and all the time on email."

"That's not the same thing, and you know it."

"Susan, the project is coming along great, and most of the contractors have been selected, but a few will have to be reined in on their pricing. I'm headed back to Belle Cove next week to begin. Don't worry, all the bases are covered."

"Since when have I ever worried about you on a project? It's your personal life I'm concerned about."

"I'm fine. I told you, dating is not a priority right now. Work comes first."

"I know what you said, but that's not the issue. It's more what you haven't said." Susan sat down. "Are you sleeping any better?"

"No."

Since telling Logan about her parents' deaths, Dakota had been plagued with nightmares. She had only confided in Susan since they began two weeks ago. What she had not told Susan was that at times they were pretty harrowing.

"Don't you think it would be a good idea to talk to

someone? A therapist, or a grief support group? It could help."

"Suzy, I appreciate your concern, believe me—"

"But butt out," she finished for her.

Dakota chuckled. "I wasn't going to say that. I was going to say that I'll think about it after Belle Cove's complete."

"Fair enough." Susan stood up. "I'll let you get back to work."

"Thanks," Dakota replied. After a few minutes of work, she leaned back in her chair. She closed her eyes and took a few deep breaths to relax. Unable to help herself, she thought about the night she went over to Logan's house, and then the dinner at Norma Jean's. It was the last time she had seen him.

They had made a lot of progress since then: talks on the phone and conversations through email, but if he saw her in person, he would ask why she looked like the walking dead, and she was not ready to discuss her bad dreams. She would get a handle on whatever this was by herself. Logan had offered to be there whenever she needed a friend or confidant, but Dakota felt unable to take him up on that offer. Despite what Susan hinted at, she was not punishing him for deserting her. However, Dakota was unable to completely trust him or let her guard down. Not yet.

Why did everything have to be so complicated?

"Dude, it's not that complicated a plan," Adrian told Logan over the phone. "You get up, go over there and see what the hell is going on. You haven't seen Dakota in almost three weeks. After the night at your apartment you told me about, and dinner at Mom's, I'd have thought things would've progressed a lot further than this."

"How do you think I feel?" Logan said impatiently. He

stared out the window of his condo, praying for patience. "She's back to emails and phone calls. Not exactly what I had in mind."

"Yeah, well you haven't exactly pressed the issue, have you? How can you not see someone you're crazy about for that amount of time?"

"I don't want to push her, Adrian. It was hard enough for her to open up to me like that. The last thing I want to do is pressure her to do anything—plus she's been working hard on Belle Cove. I'm the one who needs to practice patience right now, not go barging into her office beating my chest and demanding that we move things along. You know Dakota. If I tried that, she'd tell me where I could stick that testosterone, and that would be it. Game over. Done."

"I so don't miss the dating scene," Adrian said drily. "It's way too much work."

Logan snorted. "And marriage isn't?"

"In some ways it is, but the fringe benefits far outweigh the negatives." He grinned.

Logan leaned back and stared at the ceiling. "Don't remind me."

"So what are you going to do next?"

"Hell if I know."

They were silent for a while before Adrian snapped his fingers. "I've got it. It's a perfect idea. It's sentimental, thoughtful and will definitely appeal to her feminine froufrou side."

Sitting up, Logan arched an eyebrow. "Froufrou?"

"Hey, do you want my help or don't you?" Adrian asked.

Logan chuckled. "Yes, I'd like your help. Now what did you have in mind?"

Chapter 11

Running in four-inch heels was always a dicey proposition, but Dakota had been willing to take the risk in order to catch the Metra commuter train about to leave Union Station. Her afternoon meeting with Nancy had run over. Normally, it was not a big deal because she had her car, but this time Nancy was extra chatty, and Dakota was not able to interject a word in until the very end. After that, she hightailed it to the station.

She was on the track and had to run to catch the Milwaukee District North train before it left. Unable to take the strain, her heel broke right before she reached the door. She bent down, picked up her shoe and hobbled up the steps. Winded, sweaty and off balance, Dakota made her way to the first available seat.

There were eight stops before the Glenview Metra station. That gave her some time to close her eyes and get herself together. Or at least to make it seem like she had not just run a race.

When the train arrived in Glenview, Dakota carefully descended onto the landing. It was mid-November, and the ground was far too cold to walk in her bare feet. It took a while, but she slowly made it to her parked car. Never happier to see anything, she gratefully got in and ceremoniously dumped both shoes on the passenger-side floor, then started the car.

Once it warmed up, she turned the floor vents on to heat up her feet, and then drove home. When she got there, she dropped her purse on the table and went straight to her bedroom to undress and shower.

Thirty minutes later, she hovered in front of her fridge surveying its contents. She was hungry, but did not have the energy to fix a meal. She was pondering a bowl of cereal when her doorbell rang. She eyed the clock on the stove before going to the door. Turning on the porch light, she peered through her glass door.

She opened it and greeted the delivery man standing there with his arms laden with a large box.

"Miss Carson?"

"Yes, that's me."

"Delivery for you."

Taking the box, she set it on the floor in front of her to sign his ledger.

After giving him a tip, Dakota shut the door and took her large parcel to the table. It was open at the top, so she began taking several bags out. There was a note, so she read that first.

Dakota,
I hope you're hungry. I've ordered dinner for you with a few other goodies. I hope you're doing well. Good luck at Belle Cove. I've got a business trip early next week, but should be in Jamaica by Thursday. I miss you, Koty.
Logan.

Setting the note on the table, she peered into the first bag and then eased a covered container out. Instantly, her sour mood had been lifted. Logan had sent her a Creole feast. She had jambalaya, Maque Choux, Cajun onion rings and baked bread.

For dessert, there was a box of six designer cupcakes.

"Wow," she said excitedly. "This is a feast."

Dakota strode over to her cell phone and dialed Logan's number. When he picked up, she said without preamble, "You're going to get over here and help me eat all this."

His warm chuckle caressed her ear. When he spoke, there was still a hint of his amusement.

"That wasn't my intention when I sent dinner over. I know you've been working hard, Dakota. It's Friday, and I just wanted to make sure you had a great meal tonight, and that you knew someone close by was thinking about you. Well, not just someone…me."

"Thank you, and Logan, I would be honored if you would come over and join me for dinner. There's no way I can eat all this alone. There's enough food to feed an entire Pee Wee Soccer team…and their parents."

"I would love to come over for dinner. I'll see you shortly."

Dakota hung up and took the food into the kitchen. She placed each dish in a separate glass container, wrapped them with foil and put them in the oven on low.

She changed from her pajamas to a pair of jeans and a Betty Boop T-shirt that always made her smile. She reapplied her makeup, trying the best she could to hide the dark circles under her eyes and the perpetual look of exhaustion. Deciding that a ponytail would just draw attention to her face, Dakota used a flat iron to put a few bends in her hair so that she could wear it out, framing her face. Satisfied, she went back into the living room to wait for Logan.

He arrived thirty minutes later with a bottle of wine.

"This isn't your last bottle, is it?"

He followed her into the kitchen. "You remembered. No, this isn't. I've stocked it since your last visit."

"Last and only," she added. "Logan, I'm—"

He held up his hand to stop her. "Don't apologize, Dakota. It's not necessary."

"Fine, I won't. But I want to thank you again for this wonderful dinner. It was a very pleasant, much-needed surprise. Especially after the afternoon I've had."

She relayed the shoe disaster while she poured wine into glasses. She handed him one.

"Now that definitely tops the day I had. I spent two hours on one conference call with a man who sounded like Elmer Fudd. It was all I could do not to burst into laughter each time he said, 'Bewa Cove.' You can imagine how many times I had to mute and unmute my phone."

"Okay, you win," she announced, and then held her glass up to his for a toast. "Here's to those little things in life that make our days…interesting."

Logan clinked his glass with hers. "Cheers."

They ate dinner at the kitchen table instead of the dining room. She brought him up to speed on the contractors hired and other aspects of the renovation while they ate.

This time Dakota insisted on clearing the dishes and putting everything away. When she returned to the living room, she found Logan walking around.

"You have a great home, Dakota. Your style is elegant, yet approachable and inviting."

"That's exactly what I'm trying to accomplish at the resort. I want people to feel pampered, but also like they're able to just flop down on the couch and relax. That's why the staff shouldn't wear uniforms. They should wear their own clothes or just a printed T-shirt with the new Belle Cove logo. If they're comfy, that ease will result in positive energy that transfers to your guests. We're tying the new design into your mom's concept. When you're at Belle Cove, you're family."

"It sounds awesome, and I can't wait to see it. But no

more shoptalk." Logan stretched his legs out in front of him to get comfortable. "I'm curious why you've been avoiding me, and why it looks like you haven't slept since the day at my apartment."

Her expression turned guarded. "What are you talking about? I'm not avoiding you, I've just been busy, and I'm getting plenty of sleep."

"A blind man could see that's not true, and eye concealer wasn't designed to work miracles, Koty."

She went to get up, but he reached his hand out and stopped her.

"Hey, talk to me."

She sat back down. "It's nothing, Logan. I've just been working long hours trying to wrap up with another client."

"How's that going? Did you find the reclusive Amadeus Rothschild? I can't imagine there are that many in the phone book."

"Not yet, but soon."

"So what are your plans for Thanksgiving?"

She shrugged. "I don't really have any. It's hard to believe the holidays are almost upon us. Before you know it, Christmas will be here."

"How about coming to Aunt Jeannie's for Turkey Day? She's having a serious feast."

"More so than usual?" she joked.

"Put it this way—all the other dinners at her house will look like snacks."

Dakota laughed. "Thank you for the invite. I'll definitely be there."

Logan smiled with satisfaction. "Great." He stood up and then reached his hands out to pull her to her feet. "It's time I headed out. You need some rest."

"Logan, I—"

"I know, I know. You're fine."

She walked him to the door. "Thanks for the wonderful dinner, dessert and company. I had a great evening."

"Me, too." He hugged her tightly. "For the record, I don't believe you," he whispered in her ear, "but I won't pressure you into confiding in me, Koty." He kissed her on the cheek and then released her.

"Good night, Logan."

"I'll call you tomorrow—it was great seeing you, by the way. Hopefully the next time will be *before* Thanksgiving."

"I'll see what I can do." She watched him get into his car. She waved a final time before closing the door and leaning against it.

It was obvious he hadn't lost his knack for seeing right through her. When they were younger, Logan used to be able to spot Dakota in a lie instantly, and he always seemed to know when things weren't copacetic. It must only work in close proximity, because things were one hundred times worse than copacetic over the years, and he had not sought her out once.

Stop dwelling on the past. Focus on the present, and look forward to the future. It was nice spending time with him. Dakota went over to the couch and lay down on her side. She called Logan from her cell phone and waited.

"Having second thoughts about me leaving?" he said as soon as he answered.

"Ha. No," she teased. "I just wanted to thank you again for the care package. I really appreciated it—and your company tonight."

"My pleasure, Koty. Maybe if you aren't avoiding me tomorrow, you'd join me for the afternoon. It's been a while since I've actually gone out to do something fun. I suspect it's the same for you, as well."

"Now that's true."

"Great. How about it?"

"Yes, Logan Montague. I'll hang out with you tomorrow. Should I meet you somewhere?"

"No, I'll come get you. See you at…three?"

"Okay."

She hung up, and was unable to hold the smile on her face at bay. It would be nice to get out and not have to end the day eating a peanut butter and jelly sandwich because she had thrown dinner on someone's head. She hummed a lively tune as she turned out the lights and went to bed.

The next day, Dakota did not get up until after eight o'clock. It felt good to sleep in, and she was happy that she did not dream at all. No nightmares of any kind. Granted, she did not feel like she was completely rejuvenated, but it was a start.

After breakfast, she cleaned up her house and went grocery shopping. She was putting away her purchases when her phone rang.

"Hey Suzy, what's up?"

"We got it," she exclaimed. "We've got an email for Rothschild, and an address…sort of."

"That's fantastic," Dakota said. "What's *sort of* mean?"

"We have the town he lives in. It's Kennebunkport, Maine."

"Kenne-what? Well, how many Amadeus Rothschilds do you think there'd be in town? We should be able to track him down with no problem."

"Finding him, yes. Getting him to be our designer sheet connection, maybe."

"Hey, everyone has a price. There has to be something that Mr. Rothschild wants."

"Dakota, he's a mega-millionaire. What could he possibly not have that we can get him?"

"Who knows, but we've got to try. I've never had an unsatisfied customer, and I'm not about to start now."

By the time she got off with Susan, she had to scramble in order to be ready by the time Logan arrived. It was clear out, but chilly, so Dakota picked a pair of jeans, a tweed jacket and turtleneck. She decided that her "wild child" selection for the day would be the turtle bracelet she picked up in Jamaica, and decorative zebra socks. She was putting on her boots when the doorbell rang.

"Hey," Logan said when she let him in.

"Hi. I'm ready. I just need to grab my purse and coat."

When she returned, Logan helped her into her down parka.

"Hey, I recognize these two." He motioned to her wrist. "These are very popular at the store. It looks great on you."

"I got it because it had two turtles, and it reminded me of my parents."

"Oh." Logan squeezed her hand. "I think it's a wonderful symbol."

"So, where are we going?" she asked, trying to lighten the mood.

"Like I'm telling you. You'll see soon enough."

Dakota scrunched her nose up. "Party pooper."

She followed Logan out the door, and when she saw the red Porsche Cayenne in her driveway, she whistled. "New car?"

"No, I just don't drive it that much."

Dakota got in and glanced around the fully loaded SUV. "Okay, this is ridiculously nice."

"Thanks." He started the engine and pulled off. "Are you hungry?"

"Not really."

"Good, it may be better if we eat later. I wouldn't want you ruining my surprise."

"What is it?"

"Uh-uh. You'll have to wait, Miss Impatient."

"Fine, and I never said patience was one of my strong suits."

"Don't I know it? If memory serves, you were forever jumping ahead and reading the conclusion of a book I was reading so you didn't have to wait for me to tell you the ending."

"That's because you read as slow as molasses, and who's got that kind of time?"

Logan drove them back to the city, keeping up constant chatter with Dakota. When they arrived at their destination, he grabbed a backpack out of the backseat, and then helped her out of the car. When Dakota finally realized where they were headed, she stopped short. Her jaw dropped.

"Uh…what's that?"

"That, Miss Carson, is a balloon."

"No, this," she said, holding her hands in a small circle, "is a balloon. That's a rainbow-colored death trap with a basket attached. I'm not getting in that thing."

"Well, I am, and you're going with me. We'll do it together."

Dakota was not convinced. Surprise rapidly turned to worry as they moved closer.

"Logan, I don't like heights."

"You rode in my plane a few weeks ago."

"I'm allergic to hot-air balloons."

He snickered, but then stopped to hold her hands. He squeezed them reassuringly. "Dakota Michelle Carson. I will not let anything happen to you. This is perfectly safe, I will be with you the entire time, and I promise if you don't love it, we'll never have to go again. This will be therapeutic—for both of us."

Dakota did not look convinced. "Really? How so?"

"Because it's a chance to let go of all the troubles in your life and just enjoy the moment. I've never ridden in a balloon, and neither have you. It's something we can experience for the first time together. Come on, Koty... you've got this."

She poked his shoulder. "If I die, I'm killing you."

After the paperwork and safety briefing, they were on their way. Dakota had to admit that the red, green, yellow and blue stripes were beautiful. She latched on to Logan's hand like it was a life jacket and moved as far as she could away from the edges. She glanced at the backpack he had set on the basket floor.

"What's that, a parachute? You'd better have two."

"No, it's a blanket in case you get cold, and two hats in case the burners generate too much heat overhead."

As they ascended, Dakota kept her eyes on her shoes. After a few minutes, Logan eased her into his side and whispered into her ear. "Look."

When she tentatively lifted her head, Dakota gasped.

They were on the outskirts of Chicago, but she could see the skyline in the distance. The sun was setting, casting a lazy haze everywhere. The natural harmony of land, air and water took her breath away.

"Oh, my God...it's so beautiful."

"And you're still alive," Logan replied. He handed her a flute of champagne. "Here's to jumping in with both feet."

When did he have time to pour champagne?

She took the glass, and they toasted. Surveying the three-hundred and-sixty-degree panoramic view, Dakota was overcome with emotion. "Thank you for this."

He touched her cheek. "What better way to release some baggage than by taking to the skies?"

"I admit, this is a bit…liberating, and not as cold as I thought."

"That's because we're traveling with the wind, not against it."

"Susan won't believe I'm doing this."

"I have a solution." Logan took out his cell phone and pulled Dakota close. "Say cheese."

"Turkey," she said, grinning for the camera.

"Close enough." He snapped several pictures of them, and then handed her the phone.

Dakota sent Susan a text from Logan's phone with the caption, "Guess where we are?"

They landed an hour later, touching down safely.

"That is singularly the most fun I've had in I don't know how long."

"I'm glad I was here to witness such frivolous behavior."

"Are you kidding? If it weren't for you, I would have been sitting at home catching up on television shows and eating leftovers."

"I can't do much about your TiVo lineup, but I can definitely help in the food department. We have dinner reservations for Roka Akor—if you're up for it," he added.

"Sounds intriguing, and I've never been."

"Then you're in for a treat," he said, helping her into his SUV.

"Are you kidding? I've had two today. The private balloon ride with champagne, and the wonderful feeling of not having a care in the world. You gave those to me, Logan, and I'm very grateful to you for it."

He raised her hand and gently brushed her skin with his lips.

"Koty, I wish I could bring you that feeling every single day."

Chapter 12

"**Y**ou sound like you're about to lose your mind," Susan commented the moment she heard Dakota's voice over the phone. "I thought you said everything was going well? Was that an old voice-mail message I didn't erase, because you don't sound okay."

There was never a more hectic time for Dakota than the first day of a new project. She started work on Belle Cove today. It was exciting, it was terrifying, and she loved every minute of it.

"Yes, I'm okay, and you know how I get."

"Which is precisely why I'm in Chicago," Susan pointed out, "and you're in the middle of a buff group of guys working, wearing your designer heels that should be sneakers."

"Shows how little you know—I *am* in sneakers, and I might add, extremely comfortable ones. I may never go back to heels again," Dakota vowed.

"Uh…yeah, that's not going to happen," Susan said confidently.

"I've got to stay focused—no exceptions, no matter how sexy he looks."

"They," Susan corrected.

"Yes, that's what I said."

"I think you had it right the first time."

"Suzy, don't read anything into this. Logan and I have been hanging out pretty regularly. He's developed into a great friend to me—nothing more."

"I think that's more on your side than his. Logan Montague is mad about you, Dakota. Tell me you see that."

"What I *see* is that I have work to do."

"Fight it all you will, but you two have chemistry. That kind of thing doesn't just happen, you know. It takes time to figure each other out, laugh at one another's jokes, build up to the big kiss."

"Suzy, you're a mess."

"I'm not a mess, I'm an observationist. Is that a word?"

"How do I know? You're the one who said it."

"Fine, I'll leave it alone…for now. But you mark my words, sooner rather than later, I'll be getting that 'He kissed me two ways from Sunday' call, so I'd prepare myself if I were you, because I'm going to tell you 'I told you so.'"

Dakota laughed. "Okay, I'll keep that in mind. I have to go, but I'll check in later."

The plans she had for Belle Cove were more cosmetic than structural. During her design briefing with Logan, she recommended giving the resort a more natural, comfortable feel. She changed the color palettes in each building to reflect the individual mood of that space. The main resort was the first they would be remodeling. Most of the furniture would remain, but the fabrics and palette would be toned down, yet still tie in to the Jamaican culture and landscape.

Logan had assigned what Dakota liked to call a "honey-do detail" to escort her to vendor appointments, shopping or wherever she needed to go. She put the group of drivers to good use. There were times when she was out for hours, looking over textiles or ornamental pieces, and it was nice to have someone to help lug her purchases back to the car.

The best part was coming back and finding out that they looked as great as she imagined they would in the allotted space. There was no greater sense of accomplishment for Dakota than to see her dream transformed into reality.

"Hey."

"Be with you in a sec," she said from halfway under a table in the library. She had just purchased new wooden lamps for the tables and was setting them in place.

She backed out the way she had come and stood up.

"Not that I don't appreciate the view, but what are you doing?"

Dakota turned around to see Logan standing directly behind her. His arms were folded across his chest, and he wore an amused expression.

"You're back. Hi."

His eyebrows shot upward. "Hi? All I get's a 'hi'?"

"Oh, quit sounding like that and get over here."

She wrapped her arms around his middle and gave him a huge hug. He returned the embrace with equal strength.

"That's much better."

"I thought you wouldn't be here until tonight?"

"There was some bad weather heading this way, so Captain Tanner thought it prudent to arrive early."

"I'm glad. So," she said, turning around, "how do you like what you see so far?"

He glanced around, but his line of sight returned to her. "I'm loving the changes you've made. You have a unique ability of knowing what someone wants and delivering."

"Most people would call that paying attention," she said.

"That may be true, but that's an art form in itself. Speaking of art, what's with the T-shirt?"

She glanced down at one of the T-shirts she'd had made.

It was a pale yellow short-sleeve shirt that said Belle Cove, with two green turtle characters lounging in hammocks.

"That's a cool shirt. I didn't know that was at the boutique."

"It wasn't. I had it designed. I thought it would be nice to wear, especially while I'm out and about town. The staff loved it so much, I ordered them for everyone. It's great PR for the resort, and the turtles are like the ones on my bracelet."

"And they remind you of your parents," he said sagely.

"Yep, they do. What do you think?"

"I think you're as resourceful a woman as I've ever met."

She beamed at his praise. "Sweet-talker. You'll be turning my head if you keep that up."

"If only it were that easy."

Logan could have kicked himself for voicing the thought roaming around in his head. Instantly, a thin veil of tension drifted around them. Seemingly at a loss for words, Dakota just stood there staring at him. Heaven knows she looked absolutely delectable in that darn T-shirt and capri pants. The time away from her had not helped him one bit. The longing that he felt for her only increased the closer they became. Considering how far they had come since he first walked into her office, it was almost cause for celebration. She had warmed up to him, against the odds, and they were now in a close, comfortable friendship.

Damn. It was the absolute last place he wanted to be. No friendship zone was going to cut it when he could see and feel the warmth and appeal simmering just below the surface. It was a look they would share, or a touch when one of them would turn too suddenly and brush against the other. The way their eyes connected across a room loaded with people. Surely she had to feel this?

Maybe she doesn't, his conscience pointed out. Could history be repeating itself? Could he be destined to spend his entire life wanting Dakota and not having her?

No. He did not believe for a second that she was indifferent to him. The more time they spent together, the stronger their connection. He had experienced it at his aunt's house for Thanksgiving. Dakota was relaxed, even playful with him at dinner, and afterward, she had pitched in to help clean up. Eventually, Norma Jean came in and booted them out, so they went out on the deck. They were alone. *At least for a few minutes,* he recalled with a grin. It was cold, but when Dakota wrapped her arm around him and snuggled closer, his rising body temperature could have melted an iceberg.

Granted, she may have some unclaimed emotional baggage chugging along on the conveyor belt in her head, but it was time to let go. Claim it, discard it and move on. There was no other option for Logan. His future was with Dakota. Whether she acknowledged it or not, their relationship dynamic had changed, and Logan was no longer content to sit idly by being complacent and afraid to take chances. He wanted to stir things up and see what happened. An image of him shaking Dakota out of a chastity belt made him burst into laughter.

"What's so funny?"

He stopped immediately. The wide smile disappeared in an instant. "I, uh…not much. Just thinking about something."

"And?"

Trust me, you don't want to know. "Nothing. Just thinking about something Aunt Jeannie said. She's been after me to start dating again. Something about getting out there before it's too late…and ripe fruit…or something. I can't really recall."

An odd look crossed Dakota's face before she looked away.

"Oh, well, you know Ms. Jeannie. Always trying to fix everyone up."

"Don't tell me she's been pushing you to date, too?"

"Of course she has, but work is the priority for me right now. I've got to make One Eighty Renovations a success. I can't do that while constantly trying to meet Mr. Right on blind dates, can I?"

Logan was sure that darn body-sizzling thing was back again. He took a step toward her, but she immediately retreated.

"I really should get back."

Logan tried to keep his disappointment concealed. "Yeah, sure." He retreated to a lust-safe distance. "So how's work going? Have you hammered out the outstanding contracts you mentioned last week?"

"I did, and they've all been signed."

He nodded. "I've got an idea. Can you take off for a while and get some lunch?"

She glanced at her watch. "Can we do dinner instead? If it's supposed to rain later, I'd like to wrap up a few outdoor projects the crews are working on."

"Fair enough. I've got to get unpacked, anyway. See you at six?"

"Sounds great."

Logan walked down the steps and along the path to his villa. He was not 100 percent sure, but his instincts told him that Dakota was still in the same spot looking at him. His ego grew at the prospect, but he did not test his theory. If Dakota did not care about him other than platonically, she would have to prove it. That was when he decided, enough of Adrian and Norma Jean's plans. Logan had just formulated one of his own, and it was time to put it into action.

The annual restaurant week in Ocho Rios had begun, and it was the perfect venue for dinner. There were over seventy-five choices for restaurants that participated in the event. Logan offered a few recommendations, but left the choice up to Dakota. She picked June Plum, a restaurant at the Mystic Ridge Resort, a tropical paradise that offered a breathtaking vantage point of the town and bay of Ocho Rios.

While they were supposed to be looking over the menu, Dakota found herself distracted by the view, and the man seated across from her. It was way too much visual stimulation for her peace of mind. Logan was wearing a pair of jeans and a short-sleeve white shirt open at the collar. Out of nowhere she suddenly became very aware of him, more so than usual. He looked like a breath of fresh air. *Incredibly hot, attractive and delectable fresh air.*

"So hot," she breathed.

"What is?"

Dakota's head snapped up. "Oh, uh…the view. It's hot. Well, I guess a view can't be hot, but it looks hot." She cringed at how ridiculous that sounded. *Just stop talking.*

The waitress came by to take their drink orders, which negated further conversation. It was just as well because Dakota was mortified. She ordered a Jamaican Breeze before burying her head back in her menu. She tried to concentrate on what to eat, but it was difficult.

After they ordered, Logan gave her his full attention. Lord, that was dangerous. Logan had never gazed at her this intently before. Something was going on, but she would not be the one to name this strange electricity hovering over her like a lightning bug.

"So, are you enjoying yourself?"

"Let's see…I'm doing what I love, in one of the most beautiful places in the world. Yes, I'd say I'm pretty content."

"Who'd have known two months ago that you would end up here, huh?"

"Uh, you would have," she countered.

Logan chuckled. "That's true. What I didn't know was if you'd take me up on my offer."

"You came along at the right time. I was looking for the next client, and there you were."

His smile wavered before he said, "May I ask you a question?"

"Sure."

"Is that how you view me? As a friendly client?"

"No. You're more than that to me."

He leaned forward in his chair. "How much more?"

Her heartbeat raced as the scent of his cologne tantalized her nose. Her hand came up to her chest without her even noticing. "I don't know what you're asking me."

"Yes, you do."

She waited for him to elaborate, but when he remained silent, she continued eating. The moment passed.

When they were done, Logan paid the bill and then escorted her out with his hand at the small of her back. There was an unusual silence on the way home. Dakota wondered about it, but sensed that he was not up for talking.

By the time they reached the resort, it was raining. Logan parked the car and took the umbrella out of the back seat. He opened the door for Dakota, but she side-stepped the umbrella.

"I don't need it. I feel like walking in the rain." She grinned. "I haven't done that since—"

"The afternoon you dragged me to see *The Lion King* at the Cadillac Palace. When we got out, it was raining like cats and dogs, but you didn't want to catch the cab or subway. You wanted to walk for a while and started humming 'Singing in the Rain.'"

She stopped walking. "You remembered."

"Once I'd left, there wasn't much to do but remember."

In the past, any mention of his leaving used to fill her with anger, but now its sting wasn't as potent.

"I know the feeling."

"Do you?" He tilted his head to the side. "Are you saying that your feelings for me have changed?"

"Since you came into my office back in September? Yes, of course. We've reconnected as friends, and our bond has strengthened over the last two months, Logan. Wouldn't you say so?"

"Yeah. Among other things."

They reached her doorway, and she looked up at him.

"Logan, what's the matter? You've been pensive since dinner. Have I done something to upset you?"

Without warning, he backed her up against the door and put an arm on either side to block her path. A gasp at the sudden movement escaped her lips. Both were drenched by this point, their clothes clinging to them under the deluge of water. When he looked at her, the pained expression was barely held in check.

"You look troubled, Logan." She touched his damp face. "What is it? Tell me."

His hand covered hers, and then he lowered it to rest between them. "No more talking."

Logan did exactly as his aunt suggested. He showed Dakota just how much she enchanted him. Lowering his mouth to hers, he claimed her lips in a kiss. What started as a slow burn quickly ignited into a full-blown fire. When she did not pull away, Logan let out a sigh of relief that fanned across her cheeks. He pressed her up against the door and continued to sample her lips. She tasted of pineapples, rum and coconuts. To have thought about, obsessed over and hungered for her for so long made his control slip quickly.

With his right hand, Logan felt down the door until his fingers connected with the knob. He wrapped his left arm around her and opened the door at the same time. He pulled his lips from hers and stood there staring at her.

"You're so damn beautiful."

She smiled, moving farther through the door, but Logan remained where he was. A look of question was on her face.

"Do you want to come in?"

"Hell, yes, I want to come in, but I can't."

"Why?"

"Because I want you more than I want to breathe, but I won't rush things between us. No matter how badly I want to be buried inside you right now. We need more time."

"No, we don't," she said, trying to pull him in, but Logan remained steadfast.

He ran a thumb over her lips. "There's still a trace of uncertainty in your eyes, Dakota. And when we make love for the first time, it can't be there. I want you one hundred percent sure of what you're getting into because there's no turning back."

She nodded and reached up to wrap her arms around his neck. She kissed his lips. "I do want to be with you."

Logan grinned. "I know. I'm not going anywhere, remember?"

"Promise?"

He wrapped her in his arms and soothed her with his lips instead of words. She clung to him for a few moments before she stepped back.

"Good night, Koty."

Her smile was celestial. "Good night, Logan. Sweet dreams."

He bent down to kiss her a final time. "They will be now."

Chapter 13

The water was warm against her body as she glided effortlessly through its shimmering depths. When her head cleared the surface, Dakota struck out with long, firm strokes parallel to the waves. She treaded water while her gaze traveled across the beach. That's when she spotted him. Logan was standing at the water's edge. Tanned, magnificent and sure of himself. He waved at her. She waved back and struck out toward him. She was moving closer, and then something flicked across her leg. Instinctively, she peered through the water, but Dakota could not see anything.

"Koty," Logan yelled out.

"I'm coming," she replied over roaring waves.

She struck off again toward shore, and made it a few more yards before feeling someone wrap their hand around her ankle and pull downward. She yanked her foot, and kicked out with the other. She called for Logan and looked up to see him wave again, but he made no attempt to come into the water and help her. She frantically waved to get his attention before plunging into the murky depths. She fought in earnest now, swinging her arms in an arc in front of her. The second her head popped up, she screamed his name again and again. She saw him wave, and then turn around and walk away. Another hand grabbed her other foot, and seconds later, she was dragged underwater.

"No!" she screamed. "Logan! Logan!"

Dakota bolted upright in bed. She gasped for air, and her body glistened with a thin layer of sweat. The pain of her heart pounding in her chest sent waves of fear careening through her body. Her hand flew to her mouth, and sobs began to rack her body. Now that the nightmare had loosened its grip, she was able to lie back against the pillow and will herself to relax. She curled up in a ball with her knees almost up to her chest. She stayed that way for countless minutes before she had the strength to get up and go to the bathroom. There was no throwing water on her face. She pulled the wet nightgown over her head and placed it in the hamper. She turned on the shower, set the temperature and slipped into the hot, relentless spray.

Dakota washed herself from head to toe, including her hair. When she got out, she wrapped a towel around her head and body. After drying off, she padded into her bedroom to put on more pajamas. It was then that she noticed it was two in the morning. She stripped the bed and put on clean sheets before going into the kitchen to make herself some hot tea.

A clap of thunder sounded overhead.

"Great," she muttered. While waiting for her water to boil, Dakota went to get her cell phone. She took a throw off the chair and curled her feet up under her on the couch. She selected a number and then typed, Another long night.

Moments later, her phone chirped. She read the message.

I'm sure you don't mean that in a good way.

She smiled. Leave it to Susan. She typed, Hardly. Had a nightmare.

I was hoping you'd say you had a Logan.

Almost.

Seconds later, Dakota's cell phone rang. Startled, she answered it.

"What are you doing?"

"What does it look like I'm doing? Getting details."

"What are you even doing up?"

"*Scandal* marathon," Susan said excitedly. "I couldn't go to sleep right now if I tried."

"Haven't you seen every episode already?"

"So? Exceptional television programming is exceptional no matter how many times you see it. So were you drinking earlier? Is that what brought on the nightmare?"

"No, but I feel like I've got a hangover."

"Poor baby… Tell me about Logan."

"That's an interesting segue."

"Stop procrastinating. Just admit he kissed you two ways to Sunday, so I can say I told you so."

When silence ensued, Susan screeched with delight. "Oh, hang on, I've got to pause my show. This doesn't beat Olivia Pope and Fitz, but it's still newsworthy."

"Suzy."

"Don't *Suzy* me. Get to recapping, girl."

Dakota brought Susan up to speed while she prepared her tea.

"So you almost got butt naked with a hot, sexy-as-hell, gorgeous, single millionaire who has liked you since people were wearing revival disco halter tops, but then you stopped before the big moment, he went home, and then you had a really bad nightmare. Does that about recap the evening?"

"We had dinner, too. That was really good."

"Okay. I've got a question for you. Why didn't you call Logan instead of me?"

"That's easy. He doesn't know about the nightmares."

"Do the words *full disclosure* mean anything to you?"

"I'm not telling him about the bad dreams. What's the point?"

"Dakota, do you not see a pattern here? You're afraid to be vulnerable with him since he's come back into your life. You're trying to hold a piece of yourself back."

"Can you blame me?" she blurted out.

"Of course not," Susan said softly. "I completely understand your hesitation. You don't trust him one hundred percent yet. But I know in time, you will. Just be patient. It'll come."

Dakota stared at the ceiling. "I hope so."

The next morning, Dakota was putting on makeup when her telephone rang. She walked into the bedroom and picked up the house phone.

"Hello?"

"Good morning, beautiful. How about meeting me on your patio for breakfast?"

"Are you serious?"

"Why don't you come out here and find out?"

She hung up the phone and walked out the bedroom onto the patio. Logan was sitting at her black wrought-iron table, which was laden with food.

"Wow. How'd you do all this without me hearing you?"

"I'm very good at being stealthy." He grinned.

"Logan, this is amazing."

"Well, I have a confession. I know the owners, and the staff likes me."

"Is that so?"

He got up from the table and swept her into his arms. "And I told them it would make an amazing woman I know very happy."

He kissed her, and then set her on her feet. "How'd you sleep?"

"Not that great," she admitted. "How about you?"

"Well, when I did actually fall asleep, it was good."

"You were having a hard time, too?"

"What can I say, it's hard to fathom sleeping when all I wanted to do was be with you last night. The only thing better than seeing you this morning would've been waking up with you wrapped in my arms."

Dakota hugged him. "Flattery will get you everywhere."

"I certainly hope so," he whispered in her ear.

They sat down and fixed their plates. Dakota filled Logan in on the work she had scheduled for the day.

"My parents want to fly down soon."

"Can you delay them until we're finished? I don't want them seeing it half-baked. It's important they get the finished results."

"I'll do what I can, but I can't promise anything. They're very excited. Incidentally, you've got me as free labor today. My meeting got canceled, so I'm all yours."

"Really?" she said excitedly. "Hmm…whatever am I to do with you?"

"Several things come to mind, but none of them involve clothes…or other people."

When they were done, they put the leftovers away and then walked up the path to the main resort to start the day's work. Dakota's stamina, and her ability to keep her contractors on task, was impressive. Logan knew first-hand how difficult that could be at times, but not one thing slipped through the cracks.

He worked with Dakota and her team on the first floor swapping out lighting fixtures and small furniture while the housekeeping staff worked on updating the guest rooms with the new linens and accessories she had purchased. A plumbing crew had finished up with bathroom fixtures the day before, so the only thing left to do in all the bathrooms was aesthetic.

By the time they were done that evening, Logan had a better appreciation for what renovations entailed. He and Dakota went home to shower and change, and he invited her over to his place for dinner.

When she got there, Logan was in shorts and a T-shirt, with a barbecue fork in his hand. He kissed her, and then she followed him through the house to the backyard, where the steaks were already cooking on the grill.

"You decided to cook?"

"Yes. Mostly because I was sore, and didn't feel up to going out, or even down to the restaurant," he joked. "That and I wanted you all to myself."

"Thanks for helping me today. We got a lot done."

"Yes, we did. You're a wonderful project manager."

"Thanks, though I feel bad putting my boss to work."

"I was happy to help. You know, I was thinking, when the renovations are done we should fly everyone here for an unveiling party."

"I think that's a wonderful idea, Logan."

"Great. I'll get an event planner on it."

She gave him a look.

"What? Dakota, you'll be swamped enough with the hundreds of other things you've got going on. I don't want you stressed out planning the party, too. Besides, I have completely selfish reasons for hiring someone else to do it." He set the steaks on their plates. "Can you imagine what that might be?"

"Oh, there are a few things that come to mind. Okay," she conceded. "Party planner it is."

When they were done eating, Logan suggested a walk on the beach. Dakota took her shoes off and dipped her feet in the water. Logan held her hand.

"I know this very secluded spot if you want to go swimming."

"I'm not going skinny-dipping," she replied.

Without warning, he picked her up and ran into the water.

"Logan, stop. Put me down," she shrieked. "People are staring."

"I own the resort. What do I care if they stare?"

"Well, I care, now put me down."

She was laughing so hard that she got the hiccups. That alone made Logan burst out laughing. He released her, but did not relinquish his hold on her. He twirled her around and sang his version of The Merrymen's "Hot Hot Hot."

"So we go rum-bum-bum-bum. Yeah we rum-bum-bum-bum."

"Feeling hot hot hot—feeling hot hot hot," she sang back, dancing around.

When they were finished, they received a few claps and whistles from passersby before walking hand in hand back to Logan's villa.

"Thanks for the dance."

"Anytime. I'll have to go to New York the day after tomorrow. From there I'll be doing site visits at Belle Island and Belle Key."

"How long will you be gone?" she asked.

"At least two weeks."

* * *

Dakota was quiet. It was not the longest time they had spent apart, but suddenly everything was different. They weren't just friends anymore. They were an unspoken couple...at least she thought they were. Just friends did not make your blood boil with desire, or lose yourself in the way they smiled at you. And they certainly did not make you want to throw your clothes, and caution, to the wind. By that definition, Logan had not been *just her friend* since she was seventeen.

"I don't know what you're thinking about, but it's making me want to toss you over my shoulder and take you back to my cave."

"I was just thinking how far we've come in such a short amount of time."

Logan stopped walking and turned to face her. "We haven't really talked about it yet, Koty, but you and I...I see us as dating now, and I wanted to make sure you felt the same."

Dakota touched his cheek. "I do."

"In that case, I think we should seal our new arrangement with a dip in my pool. Clothing is very optional," he added with a huge grin.

When Dakota went home that night, it was with a new-found appreciation for patience. She wanted to make love with Logan, she really did, but part of her was not ready to take that step yet. Saying no when her body wanted to say yes was hard enough, but Logan was making it more difficult by always complimenting her and touching her. He made her want to drop-kick good intentions right out the window.

When he left a few days later, it was with a heavy heart that she said goodbye.

Dakota attempted to fill the void by doing what she excelled at, focusing on the job at hand. The new Belle Cove was coming into her own, and Dakota could not have been more proud. If all went well, everything would be complete by the New Year, and it would be onto the next one.

"Miss Dakota, you got a delivery," Miranda called from the door.

Dakota glanced up. "Thanks, Miranda."

She wondered what had arrived. She hoped it was the new benches she'd ordered for the relaxation area in the garden.

She grabbed her notebook and headed to the reception area. When she got there, she found what looked to be a bouquet of flowers for every hard surface in the room. There was also a small package for her.

She went outside on the porch and sat in a rocker to open up her gift.

There was a note inside that said, *I saw this and thought of you. Enjoy the flowers. There's a bouquet for every time I saw your smile in my mind.*

She opened the box to see a necklace with two emerald turtles. She slipped it around her neck, fingering the two figures. "Oh, Logan." It was such a thoughtful gift, it brought tears to her eyes.

He always thought of her, and what made her happy. She felt cherished when she thought of how attentive Logan was—and safe.

Logan hung up his cell phone. The packages for Dakota had been delivered. In his mind, he could see her wide, surprised smile as she opened the jewelry case. The urge to shower her with gifts and more was strong. He wanted to give her his heart, and the world right along with it, but he doubted she would be comfortable accepting either at the moment. Hopefully in the near future, Dakota would learn to trust in his love—and her own.

"Are you going to eat that food, or is it going to eat itself?"

Logan looked up to see his aunt Jeannie hovering over him. "Since when have I not eaten anything you've put in front of me?"

She sat down at the kitchen table. "Good point."

"Did she get the gifts?"

"Yes, she did. She'll probably be calling soon to thank me."

"So how are things going with Dakota?"

"Couldn't be better," he replied. "We're still taking things slow."

"Well, slow is better than nothing," she said excitedly, a smile breaking over her face. "I thought it would never happen."

Chapter 14

"I'm telling you right now, nothing else you own is fitting into this dress."

"Good thing that's it for my lady lumps." Susan gasped as Dakota zipped up her formfitting cocktail dress. "Have you got it zipped?"

"Yes. You won't be able to breathe for the rest of the night, and you may pass out from lack of oxygen, but you'll look really good."

"I told myself if I lost those ten holiday pounds, that I'd treat myself to a new, very expensive, very sexy dress."

Dakota massaged the zipper indentations on her fingers. "Two sizes too small?"

"It's not two," Susan said defensively.

"Uh-huh. You know there's a women's boutique on-site, right?"

"Yep, that's the backup plan."

"I got news for you, Suzy. The backup plan is about to become the *only* plan, because I don't think this baby's gonna hold."

"Have faith," Susan said. As if to prove her point, she gingerly sat on the bed. "See?"

"You do realize that you've got the obligatory ten Christmas pounds to get past, too?"

Susan stood up, her arms flying out in front of her to keep her steady.

"One party at a time. Let's get past this, and then I'll worry about the next big dinner."

Dakota shook her head. "Let's go."

The party for the newly revamped Belle Cove was a resounding success. Several travel-magazine reporters were on hand to ask questions about the renovations, what was ahead for the Montagues and about the company responsible for the new design. Dakota discussed the remodels and what they entailed. She announced the naming of the individual villas and her inspiration to give each a theme.

"We now have the Moonstone, Sunstone, Water Lily, Poinciana, Hibiscus and the Grande Belle. Each unique in theme and features." The columnists perked up when one asked point-blank if Dakota was dating the heir to the Montague fortune.

"Great," she whispered to Logan at dinner. "Now people will think I slept my way into my job."

"I can go on record to verify that's not the case," he whispered in her ear. "But then again, we should probably test that theory, don't you think?"

He looked so handsome in his suit that she actually found herself staring. "I agree. We should."

That got Logan's undivided attention. He turned to Dakota. "What did you just say?"

"I recommended that we test a few theories."

Logan stood up and held his hand out to Dakota. His fingers closed tightly around hers. He bid his parents and their friends and family good-night before escorting Dakota away from the group. They walked the lit path to the Grande Belle.

"I can't believe we just up and left like that."

"They'll have a great time without us, and I want you

all to myself. I can't lie and say that my intentions aren't to make love to you. That's the plan, but only if you're sure about it—about us. So what do you say, Koty? Are you ready to be with me?"

Dakota could not think of one reason to delay the inevitable. "Yes, Logan, I am."

Dakota had poured her soul into renovating Belle Cove. It was too regal to begin with, but she had added an ease of being that was not there before. There were little touches everywhere that invited someone to envelop themselves in the simple pleasures derived from clean lines, minimalistic decor and relaxing palettes. The redesigned villas were the most fun for her. The Grande Belle was designed specifically with the Montagues in mind.

Richly appointed hardwood furniture with neutral fabric replaced the leather sofas and chairs, and bright splashes of color like kiwi, mango and marigold on the accent pillows brightened the room. She also used artwork, rugs and flowers to make the large cottage comfortable, yet elegant.

She followed Logan through the front door and skidded to a halt beside him. The first floor was aglow with candlelight and vases of tropical flowers. She gazed around the room. "Logan, how'd you—"

"There's more," he said, leading her to the backyard. Lit candles cast a soft, luminous glow over the pool water and surrounding garden. Soft music piped through outside speakers. The lush trees and bushes engulfed them in total privacy.

Dakota walked over to the table. "Beluga caviar and a bottle of Dom Pérignon? Logan, what is all this?"

He smiled and opened the bottle. After pouring a flute, he handed it to her. "It's for you. Besides, we're in James Bond territory, so why not indulge?" He raised his glass.

"To you, Dakota. You breathed life back into Belle Cove, like I knew you would. I can't wait for you to do the same at Belle Island and Belle Key."

"It's your vision, Logan. I merely helped it along."

"You did much more than that," he said solemnly. "You…you let me back in. You forgave me." He caressed her cheek. "I've been intrigued, mesmerized and flat out in love with your fearlessness to try new things, your ability to see beyond what's in front of you and to embrace life despite your tragic losses. You enhance the lives of everyone you encounter, Dakota." He held up his glass. "I'm just honored that you're in mine."

She touched her glass to his. "Cheers."

"Cheers," he replied.

They sipped the bubbly and had some of the caviar.

"Thank you so much, Logan. But you didn't have to do all this."

"Yes, I did. May I have this dance, Miss Carson?"

"You may, Mr. Montague."

Logan set their glasses down and held his hand out. She placed her hand in his and moved into his arms. They swayed in time to the music playing softly overhead.

With a flair, Logan dipped Dakota before taking her in his arms again. "You're so beautiful, Koty."

The way he said it made her tingle. She leaned in and kissed him. "Thank you, but how'd you set all this up? You were with me most of the day."

"I've got friends in high places."

Dakota tilted her head to the side. "Miranda helped, didn't she?"

"I can neither confirm nor deny the allegations."

"Is that so? Well, I think I might be able to wheedle it out of you."

His eyes darkened with desire. "I don't doubt it." Logan

picked her up. "In fact, I'm looking forward to the whee-dling."

He took Dakota upstairs to the master bedroom.

"It's dark. I'm surprised you didn't have candles going," she teased.

"You and I ending up here wasn't a forgone conclusion, you know. Besides, I didn't want to mess around and burn the house down. Not after all your hard work." He grinned.

"What am I going to do with you?"

He set her on her feet, held her face between his hands and gently kissed her. "I have some ideas."

Logan kissed Dakota on her neck, letting his hands roam over her body. He moved around to stand behind her. His fingers poised on her dress zipper. "May I?"

She leaned into his touch. "Please do."

Expecting to feel a little nervous, Dakota was not pre-pared for the rush of longing that infused her when he unzipped her dress. His hand slid inside the garment to touch her back. Next, Logan caressed her skin with soft, circular strokes. After a few moments, he used both hands to ease her dress off her shoulders before kissing her right shoulder blade.

Dakota turned around and then wrapped her arms around his neck. She kissed him again before lowering her hands to his shirt, unbuttoning it. "My turn," she said, easing the material away from his body.

Unable to help herself, her fingers fluttered across his chest. The muscles underneath were hard and firm. Next, her fingers moved to the buckle on his pants. She made quick work of getting the clothing off. Soon they were standing together in their underwear. Emboldened, Dakota reached around and unhooked her bra. She was completely nude before he had uttered a word.

"You're the sexiest best friend I've ever had."

She lay back on the bed, motioning for him to follow. "I feel the same way."

Logan lay down beside her. He traced the lines of her body with his hands, as though committing every curve to memory. When he was done with his exploration, he rested the palm of his hand on her heart.

"Do you know how long I've dreamt of this, Koty? Since before I went off to college."

"I just… I still can't believe that you didn't say anything," she whispered. "All those years lost…we can't get them back."

"True, but we're here now, Dakota. I'm here, and I'll always be here. I promise."

"Don't," she said, suddenly sitting up. "No one knows what the future holds. I found that out the hard way."

"You're right." He sat up and faced her. "But what I do know is that with you…like this…it's where I want to be, Dakota. I'll always want you. That won't ever change."

A dark, looming memory wove its way into her consciousness. She moved a few inches away from him. Her stomach tightened in dread as she recalled in perfect clarity a day she had implored herself to forget.

"Are you sure?"

Logan looked confused. "Am I sure? Yes."

The painful reminder took hold, its talons reaching out to crush her idyllic notions of the bond they shared—of his words of dedication.

"You said you always wanted me. Was that true when you went to college?"

"Koty, this is a strange detour from the path we were on moments ago, isn't it?"

"I need to know, Logan."

"Yes. Dakota, I've never not wanted to be with you. Even before I left, you were always on my mind. Why are you asking all this now?" He leaned in to kiss her neck. "I'd much rather show you what I feel about you."

"No. Please, I...I can't." She hopped off the bed, and started retrieving her clothes.

"Wait, what's going on? Did I miss something?" Logan got up and stepped back into his boxer briefs. He strode over and took hold of Dakota's arm. "Will you stop for a minute and tell me what's got you upset?"

"It's not you," she said, putting her dress on. "I'm sorry, Logan. I...I'm not trying to punish you or anything. It's just that—"

"Punish me? For what? Dakota, this isn't making sense. Stop and talk to me."

"No, I'm going to go. I'm sorry for...for starting something I can't finish. Please understand."

"I *don't* understand, Dakota," he said impatiently. "Any of this."

She grabbed her shoes and ran down the steps. She was out the door and running down the path when she heard Logan calling her name. She followed the path, and eventually ended up at the beach. Dakota was dismayed to find the festivities were still in full swing. She was hoping that it would be deserted, but no such luck.

Spotting the Cabana Bar, Dakota walked over and ordered a Jamaican Rum Punch. She sat on a chaise lounge away from the partyers and stared out at the water.

By the time Susan found her, Dakota had lost count of how many drinks she'd consumed.

"Having a one-man party?"

"It would seem so," Dakota slurred.

"How'd you get here?"

"Me tek di path to di left, me stay pon it gwen buk upon di beach, mon."

Susan sat on the bottom of Dakota's lounger. She stared at her friend with amusement.

"You did what?"

"Di beach. Me pon di beach."

"What's the matter with Miss Dakota?"

Miranda hovered over them.

"Randa!" Dakota said, getting up. She weaved, but corrected herself.

Susan glanced up at Miranda. "Someone's been drinking rum punches—lots of them."

"Are you okay, miss?"

"Fugit it." She took a sip of her drink. "Ev'ryting rahtid."

Miranda's eyes widened in surprise. "Me see Tandie's been busy. Me goin' have him backside. Let's get you home, Miss Dakota."

"No, I want to dance. Feeling hot hot hot."

She was laughing and swaying to the imaginary music. She spun around, and landed right in Logan's arms.

"Why is the world spinning?" she exclaimed, overly loud.

When Dakota looked up to see who caught her, her smile faded. "Backside."

Miranda hid her smile behind her hand. "Me goin' take Miss Dakota home."

Logan straightened Dakota in his arms. "Thanks Miranda, but I'll take her."

"No, me wanna be pon di beach," Dakota protested, but Logan did not release her arm.

"Good night, ladies. Thanks for keeping our party girl safe. Time to go, Koty."

She let out a few unladylike expletives, but allowed Logan to guide her back down the path.

"I don't envy her headache in the morning," she could hear Susan say to Miranda.

"Me not envy Tandie," Miranda replied.

Chapter 15

Logan had expected to find Dakota in her villa so they could talk about what was bothering her. What he did not expect was to find her twirling around dancing with no music within earshot, drunk and cursing him out in Jamaican slang. It was the funniest thing he had seen in quite a while, but he was also concerned about Dakota. He could not understand how they had gone from almost making love, to him holding her hair while she emptied the contents of her stomach into the toilet.

From there, he convinced her to allow him to help her take a shower.

She allowed it, but flatly refused to let him dry her off. He hovered nonetheless, just in case she spun around, lost her balance and fell. There were way too many hard surfaces in the bathroom for him to feel comfortable leaving her alone.

He let her pick out her pajamas and then helped her into bed. Dakota never ceased to amaze him.

"I'm going to make something to help settle your stomach."

"Yeah? Oooh. I hope it's got Ja…Ja'rum in it. I love that stuff."

Logan did not have everything he needed, so he called Miranda, and she had an employee get the ingredients from the restaurant.

When he was done, he brought a tray in her room and sat on the bed.

"What's this?"

"A few things to ensure you don't feel like crap in the morning." He handed her a piece of toast and a glass.

"That looks weird," she said, eyeing the green beverage suspiciously.

"I know, but trust me, it'll make you feel better."

She followed his instructions then lay back against the pillows. "Is your head spinning? Because my head's spinning?"

"It will stop soon," he told her. "Dakota...do you remember leaving my place?"

"Of course I remember," she said in a huff. "Like I was going to stay with your mind on someone else. Uh...I don't think so."

"What? Dakota, I don't know what you're talking about."

"I saw you once with that girl. I'm not falling for that again, Logan. I'm not *other woman* material."

Logan grew more confused the longer the conversation went on.

"There wasn't another woman at my villa, Dakota. Just you and me."

"No," she said, suddenly agitated. "She's in here." She pointed her finger at his chest.

"You loved her."

"Dakota, the *only* woman I have ever loved, as a teenager or an adult, has been you."

"No," she cried. "That's not true. I saw you with her in your dorm room. Your friend took me upstairs, and yep. You were. You were making love with her. I left. Don't tell me I never visited you. I did." She laughed. "And look what happened. No, thanks. I won't be visiting you again."

She pulled the covers up and turned over. She was quiet for a few moments before she whispered, "You broke it."

"What did I break?"

She rolled over again, her eyes misty with unshed tears. She took his palm and placed it flat on her chest. "You broke this." She lay back and closed her eyes, his hand still against her heart.

"It can't be fixed," she murmured.

Logan sat on the edge of the bed in shock.

She yawned. "Room's still spinning."

Dakota drifted to sleep. Logan lost track of how long he sat there watching her before he got up and went into the living room. He sat down on the couch and placed his head in his hands. It was hard enough dealing with the fact that Dakota had come to see him, and had left without him knowing. But having to hear her admit that she saw him in bed with another woman when she got there was what did him in. He had no idea who, or when it was, either.

From what he could piece together from their conversations at his apartment in Chicago, earlier that night at his villa and now, the puzzle was beginning to make sense. She had done the only thing he had ever wanted. She loved him, had chosen to be with him, and he had foolishly walked away. It was there all along, but he had been too self-absorbed to see the gift she offered was beyond friendship. Beyond words. It was the kind of bond that forever was forged from—and love.

He had foolishly let himself be governed by self-doubt and fear. She offered him the world, and he had blown it.

Dakota opened her eyes to see sunlight flooding her room. She blinked a few times and then eased into a sitting position.

"Good morning," Norma Jean said from the doorway. She brought over a tray laden with food and set it on Dakota's lap. "How are you feeling?"

"Uh…okay," she replied. "My mouth feels like I slept with cotton in it all night, but at least I don't have a headache."

"You can thank Logan's quick thinking for that. He gave you a hangover drink that's been used in our family for centuries."

Dakota looked up. "Centuries?"

"Oh, yes. It's well renowned in the Montague family. Anyway, you'll be feeling just fine once you put some food in your stomach. I made mango pancakes, bacon and eggs, or if your stomach isn't up to it, just some grits."

"I'm fine. Whatever was in the drink Logan gave me last night worked. I'm steering clear of Jamaican punch from now on. Who knew they would be so potent?"

"They are if you drink a pitcher of them," Norma Jean pointed out. "From what I hear, you had an interesting time at the beach."

Dakota put her hands to her face. "That bad? I hope I didn't embarrass anyone."

"Nonsense," Norma Jean said. "Don't go making excuses for having yourself a good time. I heard you cursed Logan out, too. He cornered Tandie last night about him teaching you a few colorful metaphors."

"I hope he wasn't too hard on Tandie. I didn't learn any bad words from him. Actually, I picked up a few from the guys working on the resort." She laughed. "They didn't always know I was around."

Dakota took a bite of the pancakes. "Ms. Jeannie, these are heavenly. You've outdone yourself."

"I'm glad you like them, honey."

"So where is Logan, anyway? I was hoping he could join me for breakfast. I think I owe him an apology, too." She put her hand over her eyes. "I'm so embarrassed. He came down to the beach to get me, and managed to get me home. I hope I didn't cause too much of a scene."

"Of course you didn't, and Logan…he's not here."

"Not here? Where'd he go?"

"He said he had an appointment this morning in Montego Bay. He left hours ago."

"I don't remember him mentioning he was taking a trip anywhere. I'm surprised he didn't wake me up to tell me."

"He asked that nobody disturb you, sweetie. He wanted you to get some rest. He did ask me to give you something, though."

Norma Jean left the room, but returned moments later. She handed Dakota an envelope. Her name was on the front in bold handwriting.

"He wrote me a letter?"

Norma Jean leaned in to kiss Dakota on the cheek. "I'll let you finish eating and read that. I've got to go check on Cliff. Earlier he was trying his hand at a boogie board. Lord, Cliff doesn't even know what that is, let alone how to use one. He roped some poor little boy into showing him. I'd better go make sure he hasn't been rolled out to sea on that darn thing."

Dakota smiled. "Thanks, Ms. Jeannie, for breakfast. It was wonderful."

She beamed at the praise. "You're welcome. I'll catch up to you later."

With a wave and a smile, Norma Jean was gone. Dakota turned her attention back to the envelope in her hand. She opened it.

Koty,
I hope this letter finds you feeling much better. I
should have warned you that those Jamaican punches
have a kick. I have some things to sort out in my
head. I'll be back later today.
Logan.

Dakota read the letter twice. Her stomach twisted in
nervous knots. Dakota's cell phone was not on her nightstand. She got out of bed and went into the living room.
Retrieving it from her purse, she called Logan. It rang a
few times before voice mail picked up.

"Logan, it's me. I just got your note. Call me, please.
We need to talk."

Dakota threw on some clothes and cleared away her
breakfast dishes. While she worked, she tried in vain to
remember what had transpired the night before. She recalled bits and pieces, but nothing that would lead to Logan
disappearing on her.

Antsy, she grabbed her purse and went outside. She took
the path directly to the Grande Belle. The door was open
so she walked in. She knew he was gone, but still called
out, "Hello? Is anybody here?"

It looked exactly like it had last night when she arrived.
Still bedecked with candles, though unlit, and flowers. Except now it was eerily quiet. She went upstairs to his bedroom. She stood at the entryway, able to recall that they
had almost made love in his bed, but then she had gotten
upset and left. *You ruined what could have been an ex-
traordinary night.*

Their conversation replaying in her head, she tried to
recount the details of what they discussed at her place, but
nothing came to mind. Distressed, she left and walked up
to the main building.

She found Susan, Adrian and Milán heading to the beach.

"Hey," she said, running up to them.

"There you are." Susan hugged her. "I just knew you'd be sleeping in today—for one reason or another," she said slyly.

"Not exactly. Logan made me some weird concoction—"

"The hangover drink," Adrian supplied. "Boy, that thing has gotten me through many a rough morning." He chuckled.

"It works," Dakota agreed. "And Ms. Jeannie made me mango pancakes and—"

"Whoa, what?" Adrian interrupted again. "Mom made *you* pancakes this morning?"

"Yes. Why?"

"Exactly what I'd like to know. She didn't offer to make me breakfast."

Milán's eyes went heavenward. "Sweetheart, this isn't about you."

"I'm just saying. Mom could've hooked us up with pancakes, too. Especially since she knows they're one of my favorites, and—"

With a loud sigh, Milán switched to Spanish and had a very fast dialogue with her husband. Adrian replied back, and then turned to Dakota.

"I apologize for my outburst. You were saying?"

"Oh, I was just looking for Logan this morning, but he's not here. He left a note…and Ms. Jeannie said he left early to go to Montego Bay."

"Montego Bay?" Susan exclaimed. "Why?"

"Maybe it was to get something for the resort, or a meeting or something," Milán reasoned.

"Or maybe it was to get away from me."

Susan eyed Dakota more closely. "Why would he want that? You two were fine when he came to get you last night. He didn't look upset about anything, Dakota. Even when you drunkenly cursed at him...in Patois."

"You know Patois?"

"Adrian," Milán said impatiently.

"What? I'm just asking."

"Not now. Can't you see Dakota's upset?"

"He said I told him some things last night that honestly, I can't remember. Whatever I said, it was about what happened years ago."

"Great, more lady baggage," Adrian muttered.

Susan glanced at him. "What's that supposed to mean?"

"You know, if women would just speak up and say what's on their mind—when it actually occurs, and not weeks, months or even years later—you could save yourselves, and men, a lot of trouble."

"But I've told him everything," Dakota said. "I told him how I felt after he left, about my parents dying and the guilt I felt—how much I blamed him for my pain. He and I talked about it months ago. We cleared the air. There's nothing left."

"Not necessarily."

Dakota turned to Susan. "What do you mean?"

"You didn't mention...you know."

"Know what? There isn't anything that..." Dakota's voice dropped off. She glanced at Susan. "His dorm."

Adrian and Milán glanced between the two. "What happened there?" he asked.

"I went to see Logan. It was a surprise. He wasn't alone."

"Oh," Adrian replied. After a moment, his expression changed. *"Oh."*

"So that's what you told him last night?" Susan shook

her head. "In an alcohol-induced confession? That wasn't a good idea."

"I've got to go."

They watched Dakota run into the resort.

Milán turned to Adrian. "Do you think they'll work it out?"

"I don't know, baby, but I'm glad I'm not single anymore."

"Hey," Susan said indignantly.

"Miranda," Dakota said breathlessly. "Do you know where I can find Logan?"

"He went to Montego Bay, Miss Dakota. He has friends living there."

"Did he say when he'd be back?"

She shook her head. "Why? Is everything irie?"

"No, Dakota said worriedly. "Me naw irie."

Miranda asked another woman to cover her for a moment and then stepped around the desk. She motioned for Dakota to follow her.

They went outside and sat on the bench swing.

"What's happen that has you in such distress?"

"It's a long story, and I've got to find Logan and talk to him."

"We got time for di short version. Spill dem beans."

Dakota told her the gist of her troubled past with Logan. Miranda knew some things, but she was shocked to hear that Logan had left without telling Dakota where he went, or when he'd be back.

"And he's not answering his phone?"

"No, I've called several times. It's off."

"That's not like him. Me say we gotta give him space right now. He going through something, and he gotta work it out for himself, but don't you worry your head, now. He be back. He loves you. Me see it in his eyes. He'll set things right. And when he does, you knock him on his backside for worrying you dis much."

Dakota hugged the sage woman. Not content just sitting around, though, she stood up and said, "How do I get to Montego Bay?"

Chapter 16

"Logan, honey, can I get you anything else?"

"No thanks, Natalie. I'm good."

Logan sat back in his chair overlooking the water. For the first time that day, he felt calm and relaxed. She sat down next to him. Her smooth, dark brown skin had minimal lines, despite her age. Her colorful, flowing dress billowed around her legs at the breeze picking up.

"Thanks for letting me stop in—especially on such short notice."

"Nonsense, we're happy to see you no matter what kind of notice," she assured him.

He closed his eyes and listened to the birdsong all around him. He loved Jamaica. It was like no other place he had traveled to. It called to him in a way he had never experienced before. When he was here, he felt at peace. Relaxed and happy. That was a completely different feeling from when he sat back after hearing the words that slipped from Dakota's mouth the night before. Logan could not believe his ears. She had visited him one of the brief times that he returned to Chicago. She was there, and she had not said one word to him or his parents about it. Even when he had accused her of not caring enough about him to come visit. Not once had she corrected his assumptions—or confessed what she had seen. And to find out last night…after so much time had passed, and not even by a fully coherent Dakota…it felt like he had been sucker-punched in his gut.

"Where are you?" Natalie asked.

Logan snapped out of it. "I'm here."

"No, you were far away."

"Sorry, Nat. I just…it's a lot to process. I've been beating myself up for so long about her that it's second nature to me. Everything is always my fault, something that I have to fix. It's tiring, you know? And then I found out another thing she neglected to tell me. I just…I don't know how I'm supposed to react to this—how much more I can take."

"In my experience, your heart usually governs how you'll handle a thing. Sure, your mind tries to offer input, but it's your emotions that run the show." She leaned toward him and took his hand in hers. "At least for women."

"Clearly," he said drily.

"So what are they both saying to you, Logan?"

He pondered Natalie's question.

"Hey," a man's voice boomed from the house.

"Yes, my love?" Natalie called back.

"We've got company."

Logan turned to Natalie. "You two were expecting company?" He stood up. "I'm so sorry to intrude. I had no idea—"

"Nonsense," she told him. "You'll stay right here." She stood up, linked her arm in his and started walking to the house.

When Logan saw who it was, he stopped. Natalie turned to him in question.

"What's the matter, Logan?"

"It appears that the object of my desire has materialized."

Natalie grinned. "This is her? Oh, honey, she's beautiful."

His expression was grim. "Yes, she is."

"Look who I found," Nigel Russo said. "Dakota Carson, may I present my wife, Natalie."

Dakota walked forward and shook her hostess's hand.

"A pleasure, Dakota," Natalie said. "I see you've met my amazing husband."

"Yes, I have. I'm sorry to intrude."

Natalie went over and linked arms with her husband. "Apologies seem to be the order of the day, but definitely not needed."

Nigel kissed his wife on the cheek, and then she nuzzled his neck.

"Excuse us," Logan said, before latching on to Dakota's elbow and turning back the way he and Natalie had just come.

He walked them farther into the lush gardens. When they were out of earshot, he turned to Dakota. "What are you doing here?"

"I…I came because I wanted to talk to you…about last night."

"I didn't want to talk, Dakota. That's why I left. It appears someone on my staff has taken it upon themselves to play referee."

He knew his voice held a tone of annoyance that could not be mistaken.

"Please don't be mad at anyone at Belle Cove. I begged them to tell me where you were. I was determined to find you, and they thought it better for me if I had a driver bring me."

"Well, now that you've seen me, you can make your excuses to my friends and go back to Belle Cove, Dakota."

"Logan, I realize you're upset and—"

"Oh, you do? That's great. I'm so glad that you're aware of someone's feelings besides your own."

She frowned. "That's a bit harsh, isn't it?"

"Keeping the truth from me was harsh, Dakota. My tone is just a manifestation of your convenient amnesia. Go ahead, tell me you simply forgot to mention it. Let's hear how your coming to visit me at college, walking into my bedroom and seeing me with another woman slipped your mind."

"I…I was hurt, Logan. And embarrassed. When I came to see you, I was going to tell you how much I cared about you, and how upset I was about us not being close anymore. And then seeing you with that girl made me realize how much I cared about you. I loved and lost you all in the same day."

Logan digested everything she said, but his own hurt and upset would not let it go. He threw up his hands. "I don't know why Curt didn't mention you were there?"

"I asked him not to. I said I'd changed my mind, and you didn't know I was there."

"Great. More subterfuge. What else is there, Dakota? What other truths haven't you told me? Have you ever been married before?"

"No."

"Do you have a child I don't know about?"

She blanched. "Of course not."

"Don't say it like you keeping secrets from me is far-fetched, Dakota. What it boils down to is you still don't trust me."

"That's not true."

"Think about it for a minute before you discard the notion as fictitious. You don't trust me not to hurt you again. Everything I have said, and done, to prove myself to you since I got back doesn't mean squat because you're just sitting around waiting for the other shoe to drop. You're waiting for me to mess up so you can say, 'See, I knew you'd screw me over.'"

Disgusted, he turned away.

"Logan, wait." She moved in front of him. "That's not what I'm doing. I know you wouldn't hurt me now."

"How can you be so certain when even I don't know it? That's the point that you keep missing, Dakota. Nobody knows what the future holds. It was stupid for me to try to promise never to hurt you again. Hell, I'm just setting myself up for failure—and you are, too. I'm not perfect. I'm just a regular man who made a mistake thinking he knew what was best for everyone, and has been paying for it ever since. To make matters worse, now I can't trust *you*."

Her eyes grew wide with surprise. "You *can* trust me."

"With what? My heart…my love…your word?"

"Yes. I do love you, Logan. I always have, and last night I wanted you, but then I…I messed up what would've been a beautiful night. I never should've left."

"Clearly I said something that reminded you of what happened years ago, and as per usual, you shut down. You know, you've kept this secret for all these years, and it wasn't even that major. How do I know that when something really serious comes up you won't withhold it from me because you're mad, or want to get back at me? How long do I have to keep paying for breaking your heart?"

She reached out for him. "Logan, I—"

"You know what, I think it's better if you leave, Dakota. I don't want to talk about this anymore today. I'm too pissed off for this to end well."

She nodded, and brushed the tears from her face. "I'm sorry," she said simply before turning and walking back toward the house.

* * *

The whole way back to the house, Dakota wiped her face, smoothed her hair and tried her best to make it look like she would not burst into tears at any minute. When she reached the patio door, Dakota took a deep breath and pasted a smile on her face. She stepped into the kitchen to find Natalie and Nigel preparing dinner. They moved around each other effortlessly, smiling and complimenting each other on their culinary skills.

"Hi, Dakota, I hope you're hungry."

"Actually, I'm not going to be able to stay. I've got to get back to the resort," she said cheerfully. "Thank you so much for welcoming me into your home."

Natalie went to her side. "Our pleasure. Here, I'll walk you out."

"Goodbye, Nigel, it was great meeting you."

"Likewise. Hopefully you'll be able to stay longer next time."

"I will," Dakota promised.

Natalie followed her out front. She touched Dakota's arm. "Are you okay?"

Dakota shook her head. "No, but I brought it on myself, so I'll deal with it."

She was enveloped in Natalie's arms for a hug.

"All will be well," Natalie predicted. "Just keep the faith."

Dakota slid into the backseat and closed the door. "We can leave now."

"Right away, Miss Dakota," the driver said, and pulled off.

An hour was a long time to wallow in self-recrimination, but then Dakota was no stranger to the feeling, or the necessity of it. Logan's words drifted through her mind repeatedly. *How long do I have to keep paying for breaking your heart?*

His words, the pain in his eyes and the emotion in his voice when he said it indicated that she had hurt him—deeply. Pain rose up and wrapped itself firmly around her heart. She had messed up. How Logan would forgive her was beyond her comprehension. All Dakota knew was that she needed to shorten the chasm that now stretched before them. It was her turn to wish for the impossible.

Three weeks had passed since the launch of the remodeled Belle Cove resort. It was Dakota's turn to feel what cool efficiency and emotional detachment did to someone whose heart burned with the fire stoked by love. The proverbial shoe was on her foot now, and it was not a pleasant fit. Logan had not called or communicated with her unless it was about the resort. It was agonizingly familiar.

"Dakota?"

She glanced up from the papers she was not reading on her desk.

"Yes, Suzy?"

"I wanted to let you know that the Rothschild sheet order for Mrs. Janson will arrive in three to five days."

"Thanks for letting me know."

Susan nodded and left. Getting Amadeus Rothschild to create a unique design for multiple sheet orders for her client had been one of the most satisfying moments in her professional career. Once Susan provided his contact information, Dakota had reached out to discuss the order. At first, he was hesitant, especially when she admitted that she was no longer working with Thompson Textiles on her projects. But Dakota's confidence had been battered over the last few weeks since her disagreement with

Logan, and she simply refused to back down and not have something go her way.

When she mentioned that another one of her clients owned an international high-end resort chain, and might be interested in their own unique brand, that got his attention. It also didn't hurt when Dakota assured him that his sheets would get the press that they deserved by being featured in an upcoming made-for-television movie. She had called in a serious favor to a friend of hers who was the set decorator for a well-known network, but Amadeus Rothschild did not need to know that.

Eventually he agreed, and invited her up to Kennebunkport, Maine, to tour his studio and seal the deal. They discussed the Jansons' Bed & Breakfast, and its current color scheme and decor. It was a beautiful seaside community ninety miles north of Boston. It was idyllic and romantic, and she would have loved to share the experience with Logan, but since they still had not talked on any topic of a personal nature, that was not a possibility. She had tried repeatedly to engage him, but she was met with resistance each time.

She was packing up to head home one evening when she decided enough was enough. She grabbed her stuff and walked out to the reception area. Susan was also getting ready to leave.

"I need you," she told her friend.

"Sure, what's up?"

"I've got a project I'm working on, and I need your help."

When she told Susan what it was, her friend grinned.

"Oh, yeah, I'm definitely in."

Logan had just returned home after a weeklong trip to Fiji. He had met with developers to discuss a possible location for their next resort on Denarau Island. He set his briefcase by the door and placed his carryout on the kitchen counter. The first thing he wanted to do was take a shower and change out of his suit.

He was just putting on a pair of sweatpants and a T-shirt when his phone rang. His eyebrow shot upward when his doorman informed him who was waiting.

"Send her up," he replied.

He pinched the bridge of his nose. Arguing on an empty stomach was not on his list of favorite things to do. When the doorbell rang, he sighed and went to answer the door. When he opened it, his jaw dropped. Dakota stood before him in a black leather trench coat and boots. Her hair was loose around her shoulders, and her makeup was perfection.

"Dakota."

"Hi, Logan. May I come in?"

Logan stood aside and swung his arm out in invitation.

She walked past him. He shut the door and followed her into the living room.

"This is an unexpected surprise."

"I had to see you."

She unbelted her coat and shrugged it off her shoulders. It landed on his floor with a loud thud to reveal a tight red dress that covered about as much skin as a towel.

It dipped low in the front to reveal her ample breasts. He stooped down to pick up the coat and went to hang it up. When he returned, he was treated to a view of the back of the dress. It had a delectable dip that stopped just above the small of her back. He smiled appreciatively, and it was taking considerable effort for other parts of his body not to chime in the appraisal of the eye candy. It appeared a plan was afoot. The question was, how far would she take it?

"Would you like something to drink?"

"I'd love a glass of wine."

"Have a seat."

He retrieved a bottle of 2007 Gaja Barbaresco. It was expensive, but if Dakota was pulling out all the stops, he would do his part.

"Thank you," she replied when he handed her a glass.

Logan sat down on the couch next to her. When she crossed her legs, her dress rode even higher up her leg. He did not torture himself with thoughts of what was or was not beneath it. A smile of pure delight played at the corners of his mouth. A seduction was definitely in the making. Logan was intrigued.

"How's work?" he inquired.

"Great. I just landed Amadeus Rothschild for my client's bed-and-breakfast."

"You have to be pleased. I know how much Nancy Janson coveted those sheets."

"Apparently, they're unlike anything she's ever felt before. I've been to his studio, and I can vouch for the voracity of her claim. They are sinfully comfortable."

"Sinfully?" he repeated. "That's a big claim."

"You should try them."

His eyebrow rose. "Really?"

She nodded. "I'm thinking of having him design a brand specifically for Belle Cove."

"That sounds like an interesting proposition. Especially since I'm looking at building a resort in Fiji. I'm toying with the idea of couples only."

She swirled the wine around in her glass before raising it to her lips. "That sounds exciting."

"Which part? The resort in Fiji, or the couples-only aspect?"

He watched her pull on her lower lip with her teeth as if

pondering his question. He was annoyed to say it, but the move mesmerized him. Good Lord, she was getting to him.

"Both."

It was time to get back in the driver's seat. He set his glass on the coffee table and turned sideways in his seat.

"What made you decide to come over tonight, Dakota? Especially looking the way you do? Were you on your way out?"

"Would that bother you?"

He smiled. "It depends."

"On what?"

"On who was with you."

"Say for argument's sake, I wanted you with me."

"Then I'd say it wouldn't bother me."

She finished her wine, and then set the glass on the table. When she did, Logan was afforded a spectacular view of her bosom, and subsequently her rear end. It was getting hard to ignore the fact that Dakota was purposefully trying to turn him on. Or the fact that she was succeeding.

"So how long will we be volleying back and forth across the net, Dakota?"

She smiled. "Not long. I came over because I wanted to apologize, Logan. You weren't ready to hear it before, and I completely understand why. Everything you said about us…about me, was absolutely right. I hadn't let go of all my animosity yet, and I should never have consciously or subconsciously continued to hold you accountable for my issues. I'm here tonight because I wanted to ask for your forgiveness, to assure you that it won't happen again, and to say that I miss you."

"I've missed you, too, Dakota. And this hasn't all been on you. I was overly harsh when you came to me in Montego Bay. All I can say is that all of my anger was not your fault. Some things I was dealing with were all my own issues, and I shouldn't have taken it out on you. I'm sorry."

"Apology accepted, but where we are…it's not enough."

Logan nodded. "I know. It was wrong of me to make you think you were only to blame and—"

"No, I'm not talking about that. It's the work relationship that we have…it's not enough. I want more, Logan."

He leaned back and crossed his arms over his chest. "How much more, Dakota?"

"I want our relationship back to the way it was. Before it got derailed. I love you, Logan. I want us to be a couple again, not just business associates."

He remained silent, so she sat down on the table right across from the couch. She leaned forward, and ran her hand slowly up his leg. Her eyes implored him. "Please. Logan. I want you…all of you."

The pleading note in her voice put a chip in the wall he had erected around his heart, but still he resisted. His hand clamped down on hers to halt her progress.

"Dakota," he said raggedly. "I can't play this cat-and-mouse game with you. I'm willing to jump into the deep end with both feet here but—"

She held a finger up to his lips. Dakota moved forward until she straddled him on the couch. Her eyes bored into his. "I promise, I won't let you drown."

Chapter 17

That did it. Logan lost all remnants of restraint after Dakota's declaration. He was not in it alone, and that was all the assurance he had ever needed. She was with him. He grabbed both sides of her face and pulled her forward onto his lap until their lips were locked together.

His hands roamed over her body, as if committing it to memory. He cupped her rear end and rocked her over his erection.

She reacted instantly to the friction their connection caused and moaned his name between their lips.

Logan was lost then. He had forgiven her the moment he opened the door, but had wanted to draw out the torture of doubt for her. It was the last childish thing he would do to cause her pain. From here on out, her pleasure was his prime directive.

He set her back on his lap, but held her tightly against him. His arms locked around her. She was not getting away this time. His thumb stroked her cheek, and then her lips. He dipped his head to kiss the sensitive spot on her neck, and was rewarded when a pleasurable sigh escaped her lips.

"Say it, Koty," he commanded.

"Forgive me, and make love to me, Logan."

"Baby, I forgive you. In fact, between your beautiful face and that damned dress, you had me at *hello,* but that isn't what I'm looking for." *What I need.* He slid a thumb across the underside of her breast, tracing the outline of her underwire bra. He knew where she wanted him to touch, but he would not give it to her...yet.

Dakota's smile was luminous. "I love you, Logan Montague."

He had waited forever to hear those words in that context. Logan closed his eyes and just enjoyed the feel of her body on his, and the words of love echoing in his ear.

"I love you, too, Dakota. I always have."

She leaned forward and wrapped her arms around his neck. Her tongue snaked out to tease his lips into opening. He gave her what she wanted, and more.

Never breaking contact with her lips, Logan got up. Dakota wrapped her legs tightly around his waist. He carried her to the bedroom, and then laid her against the firm mattress. He kissed her neck. "Koty," he breathed into her neck. "If you want to stop, now's the time."

"I don't want to stop." She arched her back toward his body. "Logan. I meant everything I said. Tell me you want me."

He kissed her. "I'll always want you, Dakota. That won't ever change."

"Then show me."

God bless Aunt Jeannie and her advice. Her words were all the incentive he needed. His hand roamed down her body as if for the first time. In the past, he had touched her thousands of times, but never like this. Not like a man touched his lover. This was new for him, and he made the most of it. His fingers drifted over the skin-tight material clinging to her body, molding itself reverently to her flesh. It was his chance to do the same, and he savored every sweet, tortuous moment of easing her dress over her head and off her body. Next came her silk bra and panties.

He stilled for a moment. Seeing Dakota naked on his bed, waiting for him with passion-clouded eyes and a welcoming smile, was a dream…his dream. The image was one he was old friends with, and the real vision did not disappoint. Then his hands replaced his eyes on her naked skin. He marveled at the feel. It was a pleasure he had always longed for, but never received. Now they were here. It was real, and Logan wanted to revel in every nuance of her body and commit each inch to memory.

Her thigh rode higher against his waist while his other hand held her leg firmly in place. When she leaned up to slide her tongue across the sensitive peak on his neck, the shock it sent barreling through his body was explosive.

He sucked in his breath in reaction. "God, Koty."

In one swift motion, he rolled over and placed Dakota against his middle so she could straddle his hips. He wrapped his arms around her to hold her firmly in place.

"Logan," she moaned.

"I'm right here, sweetheart."

His hands went up to tenderly hold her face captive. He devoured her mouth. A multitude of longing was relayed from his lips to hers. That was all the incentive he needed to end one form of sweet torture and begin another. He made quick work of removing his clothes, putting a condom on and returning to the warmth of her body.

At no point in his life had he actually thought his greatest wish would be achieved. Sure, he had wanted Dakota for his own, and had dreamed countless times of how it would feel to be buried deep inside her, but all the musings of his teenage and then adult subconscious had inadequately prepared him for the reality of the exact moment when their bodies melded into one.

There were no words Logan could remember, much less verbalize to express the emotions overloading his mind and body. Instead, he turned himself over to pure feeling: the feel of her breath as it mingled with his when he moved against her. The touch of her fingers everywhere they connected to his skin as she held on to him. The texture inside her body as it tightened around him, firm and warm. The sound of her voice as she moaned her pleasure and called his name. The urgency that coursed through his veins as they both spiraled out of control toward their release, and the weightlessness he felt as he climaxed, followed by the elation of bringing her with him at that exact moment.

Those were the things he would always remember about the first time he made love to Dakota Michelle Carson.

One thing Dakota could say about the first time she and Logan made love: it was the best she had ever had. To her, it felt as though she had been waiting for this moment her entire adult life. There were only two lovers in her past, and neither of them held a candle to Logan Montague. He had flipped the script on her limited memory of what made an incredible lover. There was not one thing he had done, said, tried, licked, kissed or stroked that had not left her weak in the knees and wanting more. Their bodies were made for each other, plain and simple. No one but him would ever do. Being well and truly loved by Logan had left her crying and laughing at the same time. Who knew that was even possible?

"I can't believe that took this long to get right." She sighed blissfully.

He grinned that satisfied grin of a man who has hit that magic spot that makes their woman temporarily lose her mind.

"True, but we're there now, so everything from here on out is icing on the cake."

Dakota was sprawled on top of Logan, her head resting

on his chest. His arms came up to anchor her to his body. He kissed the bridge of her nose.

"So tell me about that dress. Whose idea was that little piece of heaven?"

"Mine, but I got the stamp of approval from Susan," she confessed. "It was my idea to seduce you, though."

"Yay you. I'd say you did a bang-up job of getting me right where you wanted me," he said with a wicked edge to his voice.

"That was the plan."

"Well, baby, you worked the hell out of that plan, but now I've got one of my own."

Curious, Dakota sat up on her elbows. "Really? What plan do you have, Mr. Montague?"

She screeched as he flipped her under him without warning. He kissed her neck, and then moved lower. His eyes never left hers. Soon, Dakota's eyes were glazed over with desire, and she was writhing below him.

He lowered his right hand between them. A glint of purpose brightened his eyes. "Round two."

She was the first to wake up. Blinking, Dakota had to remember where she was. At Logan's condo, on the forty-second floor, with the moon streaming into his bedroom window, along with a million-dollar view of the lake and city, and her body feeling like…she did not even have a name for it.

Have mercy. The plan he put into action had her firing on all cylinders like a well-tuned race car.

If she had not been in love with Logan before she got into bed with him, she sure would have been now. She eased out from under the covers to go to the bathroom. Her body felt like Jell-O that was not quite set. She tried not to wake him, but that was impossible since she had to flush the toilet.

By the time she made it to the door, Logan's body was filling up the entrance.

"Good morning." He kissed her. "Just so you know, I don't think we've ever had a sleepover as good as this one."

She laughed, thinking back to all the platonic sleepovers they had growing up.

"Uh, no. Nothing has ever topped this one."

He grabbed her hand and pulled her along behind him. They went to the kitchen so Logan could get a bottled water. He handed Dakota one. As she was drinking it, she padded over to the wall of windows.

Dakota reveled in the feel of being warm and secure in his arms. "It's so beautiful up here. The stars are diamonds in the sky."

He came up behind her. "They're nothing compared to the beauty I'm holding in my arms right now."

Dakota tilted her head back to kiss him. With a sigh of contentment, she leaned back against him. "I could stay like this forever."

He kissed the tip of her nose. "Well I know I'd never tire of having you naked, or in my arms."

"Are you hungry? I just remembered that I didn't eat earlier. A captivating beauty came over and made me forget all about dinner."

She shrugged. "A little. I guess we did work up an appetite."

Logan grasped her hand and pulled her toward the kitchen. "I guess we did. I've got Italian from earlier we could warm up."

Dinner became breakfast. While they were eating, they sat on the couch with their feet up, watching the city lights.

She observed him for a moment. "Do you do this often?"

"What?" He grinned. "Let hot women seduce me and then eat Italian food in the nude while looking out of a window onto Lake Michigan and Chicago?"

"Yes."

"Nope."

They had a good laugh over that. When they were done eating, Logan set their dishes in the sink. Dakota offered to clean them up, but Logan refused to let her.

"It's three in the morning, Koty. The only thing I want you doing is going back to bed with me."

She left the plates where they were. "I like the sound of that."

"But first…"

There was a gleam in his eye that caused her to dissolve into nervous giggles.

"What, Montague?"

In seconds she was in his arms. He carried Dakota over to the window and set her on her feet in front of him.

"Logan, wha—"

"Shh," he whispered.

He leaned down and kissed the back of her neck, then trailed kisses down her back. Fire engulfed Dakota instantly. She leaned closer to the window, its cool surface a shock to her warm breasts. The sensation was just as pleasurable as the man wreaking havoc on her body behind her. Her arms came up to hold on to the massive glass.

He turned her around and picked her up in his arms, anchoring her to the window, her legs secured around his middle. Dakota's mind was awash with sensations coming in from all around her body, but when Logan slipped inside her, impaling her to the glass wall that got priority. It was sudden, unexpected and completely out of her comfort zone—and she loved every minute of it.

Later, he carried her back to bed. Logan hauled her up

against him, wrapping his arms around her. After a few moments, he said, "What are you thinking about?"

"To be honest, not much. I'm just lying here reveling in how good it feels to be in your arms. It's so amazing—as was making love with a view. I've never done that before."

"Me, either. That's a staple now, though." He chuckled before kissing the top of her head. "Koty?"

"Hmm?" she murmured.

"I want you to know that you can seduce me whenever you want."

She smiled. "Good to know, Logan. I may take you up on that…later."

Logan and Dakota fell into a comfortable routine over the next few weeks. Neither one wanted to waste more time being apart. There was a familiarity to their relationship that was comforting, but also characteristics that were new. It was uncharted territory, but they embraced it, as they did the holidays.

Christmas was upon them, and it was their first as a couple so they, along with Norma Jean, made the most of it. Some years, Dakota would decide not to bother putting up too many decorations, but this year that was not even an option. Christmas was Logan's favorite holiday. He gave back to those less fortunate all year round, but spreading Christmas cheer made him especially happy. They volunteered at the community center with their family and friends, at Norma Jean's church for the Christmas Coat Drive and the hosted dinners for families that needed help during the holiday season.

After they had decorated Logan's condo, they went to her home in Glenview to outfit her house with loads of lights, holiday swag and well-placed mistletoe, which

Logan used the moment he got it secured over every entryway.

"I don't think my house has ever been this kitted out for Christmas before. I don't think there's a square inch that doesn't have something decorative on it," Dakota said.

"Not true. There are no lights around the shower or bed."

"That's probably a good thing, so we don't kill ourselves getting in and out of them." She laughed.

"Although…"

Without another word, Logan picked her up and carried her to the bed. He dropped her down ceremoniously and hopped on her. Dakota shrieked as she tried to move before getting squished under him.

"You know, I think we should put lights around the bed. That way, I can see how you look by indirect lighting when I hit that spot that has you screaming my name."

"Oh, really?" she said before maneuvering him beneath her. "What about when I've got *you* screaming *my* name, Montague?"

"Hey, I am not ashamed to admit that I'm totally defenseless when you set your sights on sexing me up within an inch of my life. I'll die happy, my love." He ran a hand up her stomach, and snaked a path past her breast to her neck. He held her head firmly in his hand so they made eye contact. "Each and every time."

She melted like warm chocolate before him. They could not get clothes off fast enough, and soon dissolved into a tangle of legs, kisses and sighs.

True to her word, Dakota never kept anything from Logan. She told him about her nightmares, and to date, the occurrences of those had been infrequent. Now when she had them, Logan was usually with her and soothed her back into a peaceful sleep.

Logan was over at Dakota's house one Saturday when she returned from the mailbox with a red envelope in her hand.

"Guess what?"

"It's too festive to be a bill," he reasoned. "What?"

"It's an invitation to Norma Jean's house for Christmas dinner."

"Are Adrian and Milán coming?" Logan asked.

"Yes, plus Tiffany and Ivan, and Sabrina and Justin."

Dakota enjoyed hanging out with Adrian's friends, who were really their friends now, too. Everyone cared so much about each other that she felt enveloped in love wherever she was. Holidays were usually mixed emotions for Dakota. She loved being with everyone, but it also made her miss her own family that much more.

When Christmas day arrived, Dakota cooked a small breakfast for the two of them. They decided not to exchange gifts until after they returned home from Christmas dinner.

"Hey, you okay?" Logan asked when they pulled up outside the Anderson home a few hours later.

She nodded. "Yeah, it's just that sometimes holidays are…"

Logan cut the engine, slipped out of his seat belt and unfastened hers. He scooped her up in his arms and hugged her tight.

"I know." He cupped her face with his hands and kissed her. "If this gets to be too much for you, just tell me and we're out of here, okay?"

Her heart constricted with love. She kissed him back. "Okay."

With a reassuring squeeze of her hand, Logan got out

and walked around the car to open her door. Laden with gifts and dessert, they walked toward the house.

Norma Jean had coordinated the menu so there were no duplicate items. Everyone roamed between the kitchen and dining room setting out their dishes and preparing for the huge feast. When they were all seated, Heathcliffe blessed the food and their group, and they all dug in.

Norma Jean stood up. "I want to say something."

The entire table quieted down, and everyone stopped eating.

"I just want to say that Cliff and I appreciate all of you keeping this house filled with laughter, love and joy. I thank God daily for the health I have to enjoy my son, his wife and their amazing friends. You've all become more than just our son's friends. You all are like sons and daughters to us," she said tearfully. "And we love you all very much." She raised her glass in a toast. "Merry Christmas, babies."

Adrian stood up and hugged his mother. "That was beautiful, Mom. I'm sure everyone here appreciates how you're there for us. We all feel the unconditional love that you have for everyone around you. You'd do anything to help out wherever you can. You're amazing, Mom. Not such a good matchmaker, but that's okay. We all found our soul mates, so I guess you'll be turning in your very large black book." Everyone laughed. "Oh, another thing," he said. "You're going to want to sit down for this one."

She sat down. "What is it, Adrian? Are you okay?"

"Yes, Mom, we're fine." He glanced at his wife. "In fact, Milán's pregnant. We're going to have a baby."

Norma Jean's mouth dropped open. She stared at Adrian as though waiting for him to say he was joking. When he remained quiet, she screamed with delight.

"Are you serious? You're having a baby?"

When Milán confirmed it with a nod, Norma Jean jumped up and went to her son. She engulfed them both in a huge hug, as did Heathcliffe.

"I'm going to be a granddad," he boasted.

"What about me? I'm going to be a nana, or a gigi like Ivan's grandmother, or who knows what else, I'm just so tickled pink for you both! What a wonderful Christmas present. The best I could ever get."

"Does that mean we can return the gifts we got you?" Adrian joked.

The whole table cheered and took turns congratulating the new parents-to-be. Norma Jean brought in both champagne and sparkling cider.

"Who knew I'd find a use for this?" she said with delight. "Oh, Adrian." She hugged her son again. "I'm so happy for you both, sweetheart. I can't believe you finally hit the bull's-eye."

Adrian shook his head. "Thanks, Mom."

On cloud nine for the rest of the night, Adrian's parents pulled out photo albums after everyone exchanged gifts, much to his dismay. When the night was over, everyone left happy and stuffed, leaving Norma Jean and Heathcliffe alone.

"Can you believe it?" she said when they were upstairs in bed. "Our baby is finally having a baby of his own."

"Pretty spectacular news," Heathcliffe agreed. "Makes me think you'll have nothing to rib him about now that you won't need to rent grandbabies."

She laughed. "You're right, but you know me. I'll find something else to give him a hard time about…but not now. He's done well, so I'll give him a break."

* * *

Later that night, Adrian and Milán were lying together on a chaise longue in their bedroom.

"Well, that has to give you a ridiculous amount of brownie points," Milán told Adrian when the discussion turned to the dinner party.

"Oh, yeah, she'll be singing my praises more than you do, except when we're in bed, of course."

Milán burst out laughing, and Adrian looked over at her.

"It wasn't *that* funny, Lani," he said drily.

"I'm just kidding, my love. You realize your mother is going to be a very hands-on grandmother, don't you?"

"Oh, yeah. I'm trying to wrap my head around that next level of Norma Jean. I bet it'll be unlike anything we've ever experienced before."

They continued to laugh and discuss their baby. Adrian took his wife's hand and kissed it.

"Are you happy?"

"Of course I am. How could I not be? In six months, our little *hijo,* or *hija,* will be here in person. I can't wait to meet our baby, Adrian."

"Me, either." Adrian's hands came up around her thickening stomach. "I'm telling you right now. I'm going to spoil our kid rotten."

"I think we all will. This will be one loved little one."

"If we have a girl, you realize my mother is going to try to set her up with Gavin, right?"

She laughed. "I bet."

"I want you to know that one of the greatest moments of my life will always be the day my mother sent me you. I love you, Lani."

She squeezed his hand. *"Te amo, mi amor."*

Chapter 18

"I want you to come with me. Don't ask any questions, just trust that you'll love it."

Dakota gazed up at her office door. Logan was standing there in a suit, holding one calla lily.

"Holy cow, you look hot," she blurted out.

He grinned. "Thank you, now let's go."

"What? But I have—"

He strode up to her desk and held his hand out. When she took it, he guided her around her desk. "You're leaving for the day. We have plans."

"Logan, where—"

She did not get that question out, either. He kissed her so deeply that he had to hold her up when the kiss ended.

"Now, are you going to keep interrupting, or can we get going?"

"That depends," she said, slightly dazed. "Are you going to kiss me like that again if I do?"

He let her retrieve her purse and then slipped her hand into the crook of his arm. A limousine was waiting at the curb. Dakota tried not to ask any questions, but it was hard. Especially when they pulled up to the Montague jet. He escorted her up the steps.

She looked around. "Are you serious? Where are we going? Where's Angela?"

"She's off tonight, and the captain will be flying the plane, so that leaves just you and me."

It took her a moment, but she finally noticed the table and candlelight dinner.

"Logan, it's beautiful." She looked at him. "What a wonderful surprise."

"This is part one," he told her. "More's coming."

"But you said we weren't doing anything for New Year's Eve. We were just going to sit at home, order takeout and watch *Dick Clark's Rockin' New Year's Eve*. What happened to that plan?"

"Plans change, my love. Now sit back and prepare to be pampered."

They had a decadent meal right there on the tarmac. Soft lights and romantic music accompanied their dinner. When they were done, Dakota was not surprised to see waiters appear out of nowhere and whisk everything away. They were airborne shortly afterward.

Dakota was sitting on the couch with her head resting on Logan's chest.

"I don't think I've ever been wined and dined like this before."

"There's another aspect of that sentence that you left out."

She blushed as Logan got up, decisive purpose gleaming in his eyes as he swept her into his arms and then carried her toward the back of the plane. He set her down and opened the door.

She went through and was not surprised to see a bedroom, and an elegantly appointed one at that. There were two cream-colored fabric chairs, built-in wood dressers, a small table and a flat-screen television on the chocolate-brown wall above the queen-size bed with the same neutral color on the bed linens with chocolate-brown, gold and deep red accent pillows.

"Wow."

He slid off her jacket and then began to unbutton her blouse. He lowered that off her shoulders and unzipped her pencil skirt. When that was around her ankles, Dakota stepped out of it. She was only wearing her bra, panties and heels now. He kissed her.

"Part two," he whispered against her lips.

Making love with Logan in a private jet, midair was an intense experience. It had never happened before, and Dakota was certain that it never would again—unless it was with Logan. He was attentive and thorough, soft and slow, but at the same time frenzied. They made love in extremes that night, and when they both soared over the edge in an explosive ride that left them both breathless, Dakota was overwhelmed with emotions. She burst into tears.

"Hey," Logan whispered into her ear. "You're supposed to wait until part three for that."

"What's part three?" she sniffed.

He got up and went to the table and got a box of tissues. He handed it to her, and then got back in bed. He sat up and faced her.

"Dakota, I think life has been pretty amazing between us for the last few months, don't you?"

"Of course. I've never felt this loved before."

"I'm glad, because I love you, Dakota. There's no one in this world who can love you like I do, and I know I'd never be able to find another woman like you."

He took her hands in his. "You're it for me, sweetheart, and I want to make it official."

Logan held out his hand and presented her with a black velvet box. When he opened it, she saw a diamond ring that was so large it was practically its own light source.

"Oh, my God."

Logan held out the box and said, "Dakota Michelle Carson, would you do me the honor of marrying me? I love you, and in addition to you being my best friend, I want you to be my wife."

She stared at him, then the ring, and back again. She had dreamt of this moment so many times. It did not include a bedroom in a jet, a ring that could eclipse the sun or any of the other material aspects, but the man in her dream was always Logan.

But now that the time had come, there were so many things running through her head. It was overwhelming. She looked at him, expectantly awaiting her answer.

"Logan, I…I want to marry you, I really do. I just… I'm… I need some time."

He sat back, a shocked expression on his face. "This is not the answer I was expecting, Koty."

"I know, and I'm sorry. It's not that I don't want to, Logan. I do."

"Then what's the hesitation, Dakota? I don't understand."

She tried to explain her position, but the more she tried, the more upset Logan became. He snapped the jewelry box shut and got up. He set it forcefully on the table. She jumped at the deafening sound. He threw on a pair of jeans and a T-shirt.

"Logan, I'm sorry I've upset you."

"Upset me? Dakota, I just asked you to marry me, and you said no. Why the hell would I be upset?"

"I didn't say no. I'm just…it's a big decision, Logan, and we just got back on solid ground. Why do we need to rush into marriage?"

"Rush? Dakota, I've known you since I was thirteen.

You've been the only woman I've ever loved…and you think I'm rushing things?"

"I know you've loved me, and I've loved you, but we've only been together a few months, Logan. Before now, we didn't speak more than a few sentences to each other for almost our entire adult life. I want to be sure we're both committed to this one hundred percent."

"I am, Dakota. You're not?"

"I didn't say that. Maybe in a few months when we're—"

"I'm not waiting a few more months," he said emphatically. "I want us to start our lives together now, but apparently you don't share my enthusiasm."

She reached out to him, but he backed up. "Logan—"

"You either love me enough to be my wife, or you don't."

"How can you say that? Of course I love you, Logan. And I want to be your wife. Just…can't we give this some more time?"

"Then that's a no, Dakota. And I'm done."

She stared at him. "Done? What does that mean?"

"It means exactly what it implies," he snapped. "I've sacrificed enough time in my life trying to please everyone else—my parents and their expectations, you… I've put my life on hold to do what's expected of me, but enough's enough. I want things to move forward. I want to be with you, Dakota—for keeps—but apparently you don't see that."

"Of course I see it. I'm just getting used to sharing my life with you, Logan—with anyone. I don't think I'm being unreasonable by not wanting to make a misstep and ruin what we have. I thought you would understand that."

"There's always something to deal with, isn't there? One more trial to get past, one more hurdle to jump over. I…I'm sorry, but I can't do it anymore, Dakota. I'm tired. I love you. My whole world would revolve around you, but you won't let it. You can't trust that what we have is special. Some people live their whole lives without a love like ours, and you're willing to throw it away because you're terrified to actually *live* your life. I know your world changed the moment your parents died, but you're still here, Dakota. You didn't die with them, but sometimes it's like you forget that."

She turned red. "How dare you say that to me? I was ripped apart inside by their deaths. You'll never understand what that's like—no one will. And it's true, I did wish, more times than I care to remember, that I was with them, but this has nothing to do with that. I know what we have, Logan. But you're the one walking away—again," she accused.

He shook his head. "I'm not walking away from the love I feel for you, Dakota. I'm walking away from the craziness that comes along with it."

Dakota recoiled like she'd been slapped. She stood rooted to her spot. Her world was falling apart around her, and she was powerless to stop it. He was giving up on her...on them.

"I don't understand why you're acting this way. You told me you'd always want me, and that would never change," she said tearfully.

Logan gazed into her eyes. "I was wrong."

"I don't know why I'm surprised," she said harshly. "Indecisiveness is your forte, right?"

He took the ring and placed it in a drawer. Without another word, Logan walked out of the room and slammed the door behind him. Dakota was unsure of how long she stood there, but eventually her legs gave way, and she collapsed back on the bed.

They made it off the plane in complete silence. Logan

drove her home to Glenview without one word spoken. When he pulled up outside her house, Dakota tried one last time.

"Logan, I just don't understand the line you've drawn. Why can't we get past this roadblock?"

"You see, that's the thing. I don't see this as an obstacle. You have a fork in the road. You can either go left, or go right. One path leads to me and our life together. One doesn't. Only you can decide which one to take. I can't help you choose, Dakota."

She got out of the car and walked up to her door. The moment she opened it, he pulled off. Dakota watched until the lights were swallowed up in the dark of night.

"Happy New Year, Logan."

A week had gone by since Logan had proposed to Dakota, and she turned him down. One week of silence and wallowing in her own misery. Considering how much she had dealt with that over the years, Dakota was determined that history would not repeat itself. She had to try again. She called Logan repeatedly, but he did not return her calls.

It was time to kick it up a notch. This time, Dakota sought him out. The chances of being buzzed upstairs at his condo were slim, so she opted for more neutral territory: Norma Jean's house.

His aunt was more than happy to set up an ambush, and in fact was reveling in catching her nephew unawares.

"He'll have no choice but to hear you out," Norma Jean told Dakota. "And when he does, he'll know how sincere you are, and how much you want to work out your differences. He'll come around, honey. I know it."

That was exactly what Dakota hoped, too. In fact, she was counting on appealing to his rational side that evening.

Dakota was nervous waiting for Logan to arrive at the

Andersons' for dinner. She had an entire speech planned out, but the moment she saw Logan, it flew out of her head. There was so much animosity simmering off him at finding her there, and figuring out that he had been duped, that it gave her pause.

"When is my aunt going to leave well enough alone and quit meddling?" he said when he walked into the family room to find Dakota waiting for him. "Where is she?"

"Your aunt and uncle aren't here. They left. It's bowling night."

"Of course it is. Look, Dakota, whatever you and Aunt Jeannie have conjured up is not going to work. You made it crystal clear how you feel about my marriage proposal, so let's not waste any more of our time rehashing things."

He turned to walk away, and then Dakota's good intentions flew out the window.

"You are such a hypocritical ass," she snapped.

Logan stopped and turned around. "Me? I'm a hypocrite? You'll have to explain that one."

"I'm right here—I've always been here—waiting for you to get up the gumption to fight for me—for us—but you just threw in the towel at the first sign of trouble."

"Why? Because I chose not to jump through any more hoops, or give in to emotional blackmail?"

"What are you talking about?"

"You're holding our relationship hostage. You refused my marriage proposal because in your mind, I still need to pay for the transgressions of my past. My leaving you, my not coming back like I promised. It's all relative, Dakota."

"That's not what I'm doing. You accused me of running away, of turning my back on you, but actually *you* were the one who gave up on us, Logan. You used your family's business, work and everything else you could find as an excuse because you were too scared to give our relationship a try because you were afraid that we might fail," she shot back.

"Yes, and part of me was afraid that we wouldn't."

She stared at him in shock. "What does that even mean?"

Logan cursed under his breath. "Back then…my whole world was turned upside down, Dakota. Nothing was going like I'd planned it. My family's expectations, the decisions that I'd made for my life. None of it. You were the only constant during that crazy time, but all I could think of was what the hell I'd do if that relationship didn't work out, either. I was scared to take the risk. Yes, you have me pegged. I was a coward. I told you that my leaving was all my father's fault, but that wasn't exactly the whole picture. I lied."

"Why, Logan?"

"It's stupid to think about my reasoning now, but I just… I was terrified to run the risk that it wouldn't work out between us, and that I'd lose you—permanently. Or worse, that we would get together, but that somehow I'd fail you. I tried to forget you and get you out of my head, and my heart, but it didn't work. Over the years I realized that my not trying was condemning me to a life of unhappiness."

"And me," she said bitterly. "You weren't the only one affected by your inability to make a choice, Logan."

"I told myself that you'd forget about me, that you'd move on and find someone better for you than I was."

Tears fell haphazardly down her face. Her eyes mirrored her disillusionment.

"You were wrong."

Adrian had insisted that Logan play basketball with him. He was not happy about the outcome of that decision.

"Dude, you took sucked to a whole new level. Your mind was everywhere but that game."

"Sorry, man."

Adrian went to Logan's refrigerator and got a beer. He came over and handed one to his cousin. He sat down and put his feet up on the coffee table.

"So what have you been up to?"

"Not much."

"Have you spoken to Dakota at all?"

"No."

"You know, conversations would go a lot easier if you didn't have the cryptic one-liners for responses."

Logan eyed his beer.

"Why don't you call her, man?"

"I tried. She's disappointed in me, and I can't blame her. She's right. I was an indecisive jackass in my youth, and it's coming back to ruin my happiness now. I guess you really do reap what you sow."

"Logan, quit beating yourself up now for stupid decisions you made as a teenager. We all made mistakes. It goes along with the territory."

"Maybe it's better this way."

"Okay, now you *are* being a jackass."

"Adrian, how many times does a person need to get kicked in the teeth before he stops smiling?"

"Look, I'd readily agree and leave you alone if I thought it was what you wanted, or needed. But for the life of me, Logan, I don't understand why you're so hell-bent on letting your pride destroy your happiness. You spend your whole life pining after a girl, you move back to your hometown where you profess your undying love for her, and you say that you won't desert her and will do whatever it takes to win her back. Then when you get her, and she hesitates about your marriage timetable, you're ready to wash your hands or do whatever it takes to sabotage it."

"I'm tired, Adrian. I'm tired of me, I'm tired of her and I'm tired of us. I can't fight all three—not anymore. Enough about my problems. How are things going with you? How's your wife, and the baby?"

Adrian beamed. "Milán is doing well. She's four months pregnant, and eating me out of house and home, but if you tell her I said that, I will deny it."

Logan laughed. "I got you."

"I know I'm beating a dead horse—"

"That seems to run in the family."

"But…are you sure things won't work out with Dakota?"

With a harsh sigh, Logan bolted off the couch. He threw his hands up in frustration. "I see my friends, Natalie and Nigel, and Miranda and her husband. Those two couples have love, respect and drama-free living. They love each other, Adrian. I mean, true and deep love. They're not afraid to show it, or to live in their own flaws. It's the same for you and Milán. You all have healthy, loving relationships, but you also have a stable foundation. I don't think Dakota and I have that solid base. As much as I love her, and it kills me that we're not together, our relationship will never work because we're not standing on a concrete foundation. It's all an illusion, and it's taken me this long to realize that neither one of us can bear the weight by ourselves anymore. If both of us aren't all in, our foundation crumbles."

Adrian was silent for a few moments. "Look, I hear what you're saying. Believe me, but I know you, Logan. All you've ever wanted since you were a teenager is Dakota. You have her now, and for some reason, you're resisting it. All I'm asking is that you think long and hard before giving up and walking away. You stand to lose a lot, cousin.… I just hope you're prepared for what happens if you can't put this back together again."

Setting his drink on the table, Adrian got up. "Just think about what I said." He punched Logan's arm lightly. "I'll see myself out."

Three days later, Susan rang Dakota's doorbell again and waited. It was the third try, and Dakota still had not answered. Since her blowup with Logan, she had steered clear of everyone, which was really starting to worry Susan.

"I think it's time to use your key," Norma Jean said from behind her.

"I'd hate to use it if she's home."

"Well, one thing's for sure, she's not planning to let us in, so we're letting ourselves in. Now do you want to do the honors, or shall I?"

Using her key, Susan opened Dakota's door.

"Dakota? We're coming in, don't shoot. It's Susan and Ms. Jeannie."

They walked in and shut the door behind them. It was dark, so Susan turned on the light in the hall. She looked at the glass bowl on the table.

"Her keys are here. That's a good sign."

"An actual person would be, too," Norma Jean replied.

They walked into the living room, and then into the kitchen.

"Good Lord, it looks like a food bomb went off in here…a week ago."

They were about to search for Dakota when she came into the room singing at the top of her lungs. "When love runs out and the pain walks in, and settles for a stay—"

When she saw Susan and Norma Jean standing there

staring at her, she screamed. Her hands flew out in front of her to ward off an attack.

"What are you both doing here?" she gasped.

They glanced at Dakota's disheveled appearance, hair flying and the hair brush that she was using for a microphone, now a weapon.

"We're worried about you," Norma Jean told her. "What's your excuse, and why are you singing Bobby Womack songs?"

"Dakota, you haven't been to work in a few days."

"I've been...under the weather," she replied. She went into the kitchen and grabbed a bag of Cheetos from the pantry.

"It's your company, you can work from Siberia if you want to," Susan pointed out, "but we're worried about you."

She went back to her bedroom. "I'm fine," she said around what sounded like a mouthful of the cheesy snacks.

They followed her to the doorway. Seconds later, another sound piped over the speakers in Dakota's room. She listened to the first few verses and then broke down into tears as she sang along. "And how can you mend a broken heart? How can you stop the rain from falling down?"

"Dakota, maybe you should let the Bee Gees take over from here," Susan said gently. "Ms. Jeannie?"

"What?" Norma Jean went over and sat down at the edge of Dakota's bed. Mostly because that was the only space that didn't have dishes, food or newspapers on it.

"Look, you've got to get yourself together, Dakota. Being depressed is not going to fix your relationship. Only you can do that," Norma Jean said gently.

"There's nothing to fix," she said. "He doesn't want to have anything to do with me."

"Well, if I saw you with your hair flying, wearing raggedy sweatpants, smelling like old corn chips and looking like you've been set outside with the recycling, I'd steer clear, too."

Susan looked toward the ceiling.

"Look, there's no use sugarcoating anything. That's not going to help her. Now listen to me, Dakota. You're depressed. We all get it, but that's not getting you better, and that's certainly not going to bring your man back."

"Haven't you heard? He's not coming back." Dakota blew her nose in a tissue before lobbing it onto a pile next to her bed. "Besides, why would I want him anyway? He's a lying, spineless sack of..."

"We get it. He didn't fight for you." Norma Jean got up and cut the music off. She went over and opened the blinds. When she turned around, she put her hands on her hips. "But neither did you. You didn't barge into that bedroom and lay down the law any more than he conquered his fears of failure."

Dakota snorted. "Well, we'll never know now, he's given up again."

"Then I tell you what—you want him, *you* go get him. Both of you need to stop keeping score, and get on the same page. You start by showing him what he's missing. But first you need to get showered, fix yourself up, sign up for a few therapy sessions and eat a hot meal. Not necessarily in that order." She walked over and took the jalapeño-flavored Cheetos bag out of Dakota's hand. "Now let's get moving, honey, daylight's burning."

"You need a new attitude, must put the demons of the past to rest, and no more junk-food binges. It's time to get back on the mat, honey."

Dakota was staring out the window. Norma Jean's words still echoed in her head. Ever since the day Susan and Norma Jean did their version of an intervention, Da-

kota had been a whirlwind of activity. She had taken
Norma Jean's advice and had gotten back on the mat to
fight for her happiness. She joined a grief support group,
a gym and reevaluated the things in life that truly made
her happy. Every day was not a picnic, and her sadness
at not having her parents threatened to incapacitate her
at times, but Dakota was learning that on those days, she
had to hang in there and weather the storm because the
sun always came out.

In her heart, Dakota knew that it was the same for her
relationship with Logan. Not once had she ever wavered
in her belief that they would get back together. Her love
for him was a constant in her life, and in the face of adver-
sity had only thrived like a live plant stretching to reach
sunlight.

Today's prime directive was to see Logan and make
peace. She could not go another day with the two of them
at odds. Dakota did not know what she would say when
she saw him, but she would make sure he understood that
life was too short, and she wanted her time to be spent in
the arms of the man she loved.

With a confident smile, she stepped out into the sunlight, and into the cab waiting for her at the curb.

Miranda walked around to the small garden and sat
down.

"When you going talk about it?"

Logan did not bother looking up. "I'm not."

"How long you going be moping about?"

"I'm not moping. I'm thinking."

"Really now? What you be thinking bout—or should
I say whom?"

"Not necessary. The answer hasn't changed in the week
that you've been asking."

She smiled. "Yeah, well, the mind can't always deliver what the heart wants, Logan."

He stood up and kissed her on the cheek. "I know."

Walking down the path to his villa, Logan reflected on life since he and Dakota broke up. He had issued an ultimatum, and it had blown up in his face. There was no move left for him to make. He thought of his aunt waiting in the wings to find him his dream girl. He did not have the heart to tell her that any attempts to fix him up would be in vain. There was no other woman for him but Dakota. She was the only woman he would ever want. In fact, he had done nothing since he had seen her last but think about her. No work, no distractions and no excuses. He took a long, hard look at his life and his relationship with her from every possible angle.

She was absolutely right. He had run away at the first sign of discord. He had started ten years ago, and he had not stopped running since. All the declarations he had been spouting since moving home were just lip service. Not once had he evaluated his own actions, or motivation when it came to being in a relationship with her. He was so intent on paying for the sins of the past that he never stopped to live in the present. It took Adrian to point out that his pride was interfering with his happiness, and that he still loved Dakota with all of his heart. This was their bump in the road, and somehow the two of them had to find their way back to each other. There was no other alternative for Logan because without her, his foundation had crumbled, and so had his heart.

He picked up his cell phone, but then hung up. This was not a conversation for the telephone. It had to be in person. Decision made, Logan headed back to his villa to pack.

He walked in to find Dakota sitting in his living room. He stared as if she were a ghostly apparition.

"Dakota."

"Hi, Logan."

"I… How are you?"

"Well, and you?"

Terrible. Lonely as hell. "Good. So what brings you to Jamaica?"

"Work."

His heart fell. "Okay. What's going on? I believe you received the timetable for Belle Island renovation, right?"

"Yes, I did, but that's not the type of work I came here to discuss."

"Then what? Are you working on a new venture?"

"The kind of work I've been doing is more…introspective."

He sat down on the couch next to her. "Really? Like what?"

"For starters, I've been going to counseling to deal with my grief over losing my parents. It had been simmering over the years, but I never addressed the root of my problems over their deaths."

"And now you've come to terms with it?"

She nodded. "It wasn't easy, nor is my journey over, but I have better coping mechanisms in place now, and I'm taking things one day at a time."

"I'm glad for you, Dakota. That's great news."

"You were right. I did have a lot of baggage that I had never dealt with. It clouded my ability to see things for what they were."

"I'm afraid I'm the last person that should've been talking to you about extra baggage," he admitted. "I've got plenty of my own. I had no right to judge you."

"One thing I've learned is that love knocks a person on their ass if they aren't prepared."

He smiled at that. "Were you prepared?"

"No. I thought I was, but I didn't have a clue. It's hard to explain, but the truth is, I got tired of myself, Logan."

"Believe me, that concept is easier to grasp than you think."

"I needed to start fresh, clean house and really get to know *me*. I guess the panic I felt when you proposed was the realization that I couldn't go into a long-term relationship with you until I got my own house in order. I had to repair my heart, not just for me, but for you. I'm just sorry I didn't see it earlier. I could've saved us both a lot of heartache."

"It would appear that everything turned out like it was supposed to."

"Not everything—I don't have you."

Logan's jaw tightened. "Dakota—"

She held up her hand. "Please hear me out. I know you said that if I didn't accept your proposal, then our relationship was over, but I'm hoping that you can give us…give me another chance. I love you, Logan. I always have. That's not going to change, and it's never going to stop. Whether we're together or apart, I'll still love you. Personally, I'd rather be together."

"There's only one problem with your whole scenario," he said.

Dakota's face fell. "Okay. What?"

"In order for your revised plan to work, you'd have to agree to marry me."

Her smile was luminous. "Logan, are you sure?"

"I am. I've missed you like crazy, and I was an ass the night I proposed. My pride got the better of me. I had no right to pressure you, or make you feel like I did. Once I got over feeling sorry for myself, I came to terms with the fact that I might have messed things up permanently, but I would never stop loving you. I didn't think we had a strong enough foundation to keep us together, and I thought that we weren't as committed as other couples I'd seen, but I know now how stupid an assumption that was." He took her hands in his. "We *are* solid, Dakota, and we're stronger together than apart because *you* are my foundation, and *I* am yours. I'm so sorry for hurting you. Please accept my heartfelt apology, and say you'll marry me, Koty, and put us both out of our misery."

She flung herself into his arms. "Yes," she said against his lips. "I will marry you. Above any and everything, I want to be your wife, Logan Montague. For better or worse, you're mine!"

He hauled her up against him and crushed her mouth to his. Logan was certain that this time they would make it work. No more second-guessing each other.

Their love was by design, and would never be broken. No matter what they faced, as long as they were together, he and Dakota would be irie.

Epilogue

"I'm not about to eat some freezer-burned piece of wedding cake," Dakota Montague announced.

"Come on, it probably tastes fine," Logan told her.

One year had passed since they were married in Ocho Rios at the Belle Cove resort. They spent their honeymoon in Fiji combining a little business with pleasure. While they were getting to know each other as man and wife, Logan was in the process of acquiring an existing resort on Denarau Island. From there, Dakota would embark on a renovation to bring it up to their resort standards.

Now, one year later, they were seated at a long table in the garden of Belle Cove with their closest family and friends. With a tap of his knife on the champagne glass in front of him, Logan's father, Charles Montague, asked for everyone's attention. He stood up and glanced at the young couple.

"Logan and Dakota, to be honest, I think everyone here had their doubts about whether the two of you would get and stay together. I'm happy to say that you've proved all the naysayers wrong. Your love is strong and continues to stand the test of time. I know I speak for everyone here when I say that we couldn't be happier for you both. Cheers. We love you," his father said, his voice heavy with emotion.

Everyone raised their glasses to toast the Montagues' first anniversary. His parents had flown the entire wedding party back to Jamaica for the special occasion. Norma Jean was beside herself now that she was the grandmother of a lovely baby girl, Angelica Jean. Tiffany and Ivan's brood increased as they welcomed a baby sister, Kennedy Cecile, for Gavin. He enjoyed being the big brother, and everyone joked that Norma Jean was already lining up prospects for the Anderson and Mangum progeny.

Later that night, Dakota and Logan were stretched out in a hammock on the back porch of their estate. Logan had purchased a sprawling property a short drive away from Ocho Rios in Old Fort Bay. Dakota named it Turtle Dove Landing for her parents. It was complete with an in-law suite, but their friends and family decided to leave the newlyweds in peace and stayed at Belle Cove.

Dakota snuggled closer to her husband. "Today was perfect. Thank you for such a beautiful celebration, Logan. It's great having everyone here for a few days."

"I agree, though I would love to have you all to myself this week so I can have my way with you."

"Really? And just what would you be doing with me?"

He whispered into her ear. She blushed at Logan's amorous propositions.

"I didn't think I could still make you blush," he teased. "I wonder what else I can do to make my wife turn delectable shades of red."

Dakota ran a hand down his leg. "I guess we'll have to try a few things and find out."

He leaned over and kissed her. "I feel like the most blessed man in the world to have such an amazing wife. When we're together, there's nothing we can't do. I love you, Koty Montague. With all my heart."

"I love you, Logan, and I will forever."

"It will hardly be long enough, but it's a start," he said solemnly. He stood up and helped her to her feet. "I have something for you," he said, walking her into their bedroom.

"Logan, you've done so much already," she protested.

"The sky's the limit for you, sweetheart." He handed her a large box. "Open this one first."

Dakota ripped the paper and dove into her present. She peered into the large box and grinned.

"Rothschild sheets?"

Logan nodded.

"But…Amadeus already made some for the resorts."

"True, but I had him create *our* own design. Especially for you and me."

Dakota took the sheets completely out of the box and studied them. There was an image that integrated their initials into the design in the middle with a pattern that weaved itself out from there and back around to the beginning.

"Never ending," she said tearfully.

"Just like us, Koty."

She wrapped her arms around his neck and hugged him tightly. "Logan, I love them. Thank you, sweetheart. These were so thoughtful."

"I'm not done. Wait for it…" He handed her a smaller package.

She opened it, and then looked up at him. "What's this?"

"The key to your new office space, my love. One Eighty Renovations—Jamaica."

Her hand flew to her mouth. "Logan? What have you done?"

"It's not far from here, has incredible views, plenty of parking for your clients and is conveniently close to here for afternoon rendezvous." He grinned. "You've got room for staff, and your old renovation team is on standby. Happy anniversary, Dakota."

She threw her arms around him. "Thank you so much," she said around tears. "I can't believe you did all this for me."

Logan kissed her tenderly. "From the moment I met you, I knew there was nothing I wouldn't do for you, Koty."

She smiled in remembrance of their first meeting. "You were my hero then, and you still are. I've got an anniversary present for you, too, husband."

His eyes roamed over the slinky nightgown she was wearing. "I don't think I need a present. The way you're looking in that nightgown, *you* are my present."

She walked over to the dresser and pulled a box out of the drawer.

"I can't believe I missed that. I'm in and out of the drawer all the time." He laughed.

"I guess you're not very observant."

"That's because when you walk into the room, you eclipse everything else."

"You are such a flirt."

"Yes, but you love it."

"I love you," she said simply. "Open it."

Logan opened the box and pulled out a piece of paper with an arrow on it.

"What's this? A treasure map?"

"Not quite." They walked downstairs and outside. Logan turned it around, and it pointed toward the back of the house. Excited, Logan walked a little ahead of her. There was a small room attached to the house. His map pointed there. Dakota motioned for him to go in first. When he walked through the door, he whistled.

"It's a man cave."

He took in the pool table, a floor-to-ceiling projection

screen, projector and ample seating. He also had a bar, re-frigerator and a large selection of movies.

He hugged her. "This is amazing. Thank you, sweet-heart. I love you—and my present."

"Happy anniversary, my love, but there's more where that came from." She wriggled her rear end suggestively.

He picked her up. "You know, I think we need to chris-ten my new man cave."

She shrieked with delight as he deposited her on the couch and then joined her.

Dakota molded herself to every square inch of her hus-band. No matter where they were, as long as they were to-gether, she was home. They were a family, and they would eventually increase their family by having their own chil-dren. She thought of how happy her parents had been in their lives, and knew that she had also found an unbreak-able love that would last forever.

Dakota Carson Montague was at peace, and complete.

* * * * *

REQUEST YOUR FREE BOOKS!

2 FREE NOVELS PLUS 2 FREE GIFTS!

KIMANI ROMANCE

Love's ultimate destination!

YES! Please send me 2 FREE Harlequin® Kimani™ Romance novels and my 2 FREE gifts (gifts are worth about $10). After receiving them, if I don't wish to receive any more books, I can return the shipping statement marked "cancel." If I don't cancel, I will receive 4 brand-new novels every month and be billed just $5.19 per book in the U.S. or $5.74 per book in Canada. That's a savings of at least 20% off the cover price. It's quite a bargain! Shipping and handling is just 50¢ per book in the U.S. and 75¢ per book in Canada.* I understand that accepting the 2 free books and gifts places me under no obligation to buy anything. I can always return a shipment and cancel at any time. Even if I never buy another book, the two free books and gifts are mine to keep forever.

168/368 XDN F4XC

Name _____ (PLEASE PRINT) _____

Address _____ Apt. #

City _____ State/Prov. _____ Zip/Postal Code

Signature (if under 18, a parent or guardian must sign)

Mail to the **Harlequin® Reader Service:**

IN U.S.A.: P.O. Box 1867, Buffalo, NY 14240-1867
IN CANADA: P.O. Box 609, Fort Erie, Ontario L2A 5X3

Want to try two free books from another line?
Call 1-800-873-8635 or visit www.ReaderService.com.

* Terms and prices subject to change without notice. Prices do not include applicable taxes. Sales tax applicable in N.Y. Canadian residents will be charged applicable taxes. Offer not valid in Quebec. This offer is limited to one order per household. Not valid for current subscribers to Harlequin® Kimani™ Romance books. All orders subject to credit approval. Credit or debit balances in a customer's account(s) may be offset by any other outstanding balance owed by or to the customer. Please allow 4 to 6 weeks for delivery. Offer available while quantities last.

Your Privacy—The Harlequin® Reader Service is committed to protecting your privacy. Our Privacy Policy is available online at www.ReaderService.com or upon request from the Harlequin Reader Service.

We make a portion of our mailing list available to reputable third parties that offer products we believe may interest you. If you prefer that we not exchange your name with third parties, or if you wish to clarify or modify your communication preferences, please visit us at www.ReaderService.com/consumerschoice or write to us at Harlequin Reader Service Preference Service, P.O. Box 9062, Buffalo, NY 14269. Include your complete name and address.

KROM13R